RUTHLESS PROMISE

M. JAMES

Copyright © 2021 by M. James

All rights reserved.

No part of this book may be reproduced in any form or by any electronic or mechanical means, including information storage and retrieval systems, without written permission from the author, except for the use of brief quotations in a book review.

This is a work of fiction. Names, characters, businesses, places, events and incidents are either the products of the author's imagination or used in a fictitious manner. Any resemblance to actual persons, living or dead, or actual events is purely coincidental.

SOFIA

1

My first thought when I wake up is that my head feels as if it's splitting open.

My next is that it's freezing cold. I blink slowly, my eyes feeling sticky and glued together, and my mouth feels dry, like it's been stuffed with cotton. Pain radiates through every inch of my body, and when I move, another bolt splits my head, making me cry out.

That's when I realize there's a gag in my mouth, a thick wad of fabric stuffed in and secured around my head. I try to spit it out, my throat contracting, and my stomach heaves with nausea.

*No. No no, no, I can't throw up, I can't—*The thought of vomiting right now, with no way to spit it out, is enough to make me feel even more like retching.

"She's waking up." A voice from across the room makes me twist my head to the side, forcing my eyes open despite the pain ricocheting around my skull. Slowly, the room comes into view, and I see three men blocking my view of the rest of the room, dressed in black pants and t-shirts with combat boots on. They're the men who kidnapped me at the church, without a doubt, but I don't understand why their accents sound Italian. I can't think of any reason why anyone in the Italian mafia would want to kidnap me, unless…

"That drug wore off awfully fucking fast. How much did you give her?"

"She was squirming around a lot. We had a hard enough time getting it over her face—"

I don't hear what else the man who responded says because my head is spinning, my pulse thundering so loudly in my ears that it drowns everything else out. I know that voice. I remember the sound of it in the hospital all too well, telling me how he should have just killed me, right before he snatched my mother's necklace off of my neck.

Vitto Rossi.

I try to spit out the gag again, thrashing on the bed as I try to sit up, to get away. But my hands are tied, bound above me to the headboard, and I have a sudden sick rush of fear as I'm thrown back to waking up in the hotel room with the Russians, that brutish man's face leering over me as he grabbed my chin—

"Well, she's definitely fucking awake now," Rossi growls, and the men split apart, giving me a glimpse of him for the first time since I woke up.

He's in a wheelchair, and he doesn't look good. His face is an ashy grey, lacking healthy color. It seems to have sagged during his time in the hospital, leaving him with jowls that he didn't have before, made even more disgusting by the greyish black stubble covering his chin. This isn't the man who danced with me at my wedding to Luca. He'd been a strong and vital man then, almost handsome if not for the bit of extra weight he was carrying around. I would almost feel sorry for him, seeing it all sucked away by his injuries like this—if he wasn't set on killing me, that is.

I don't understand. I don't know why I'm so important to everyone, why I keep winding up like this, tied to beds in strange rooms with men intent on hurting me, violating me, selling me, killing me.

I can almost hear Luca's voice in my ear, telling me that I should have stayed home. That I should have listened to him. That if I hadn't left the penthouse and run to the cathedral, I'd be safe right now, locked away in the gilded cage that Luca gave me surrounded by the best security money can buy. I wouldn't be in this room, trying desperately not to throw up and choke on my own vomit. At the same time, I wonder frantically why the former don of the mafia abducted me.

Does he really want me dead that badly? I try to get a good look at the other men in the room, to memorize their faces, but they're no one I recognize. They look vaguely familiar—they were probably at my wedding and Caterina's, just faces in the crowd, some of Rossi and Luca's soldiers. Men who apparently are loyal to Rossi still, and not my husband.

Rossi wheels his chair towards me, and I feel fear start to creep through the shock, chilling my blood ice cold. It doesn't matter if I can identify the men helping him because there's no way I'm making it out of this alive. Rossi wouldn't have gone this far just to let me run back to Luca. Even if I swore never to say a word, he wouldn't believe me, and there's no way I'd be able to keep it from Luca anyway. He'd wring it out of me one way or another.

When my husband wants something, I've learned, there's no denying him.

Under other circumstances, even after what happened the other night, that thought might send a shiver of lust through me. But I'm too overcome by fear right now, not just for myself but also for my baby.

The baby. I feel sick all over again at the thought. It's an awful irony that the very thing that was meant to save my baby, running to Father Donahue for help, is what got me here. I can't even try to leverage my pregnancy to save my life because of the contract Luca made me sign.

The stipulation that he never explained. That I never *made* him explain because we were never supposed to sleep together. That I never brought up again because he used a condom on our wedding night, and we weren't supposed to ever do it again. And then—

We did it again. And again. And again. I'm not sure how many times Luca fucked me bare. Still, I know for sure that we didn't use a condom even once that entire night after he flew home from the Dominican Republic and fucked me over and over again until we were both too sore and spent to move. And I'm certain that's the night I got pregnant.

Whatever the reason is for that stipulation in the contract, I'd bet all the money I have—which admittedly, is zero that I have access to right now—that Rossi has something to do with it. So telling him that I'm pregnant won't save my life.

It'll just give him even more of a reason to kill me.

I whimper as he comes towards me, the sound muffled by the gag, and I hate myself for it. He hears it; I see the smile that spreads across his face as he moves towards the side of the bed, a truly hateful one.

"Little Sofia Ferretti," he croons, reaching out to run one hand down my arm. His palm is clammy, and I try to writhe away, but my hands are bound tightly, and I can't move them at all. He trails that hand down to my cheek, cupping my face in his palm for a moment, and I wish more than anything that I could bite him. Instead, I just wrench my face sideways, narrowing my eyes angrily at him.

"Oh, I can see that Luca was right. You're a little spitfire. But not much you can do bound and gagged, now is there?" He glances over at one of the men standing at the end of the bed, a swarthy, shorter man with a thick, close-trimmed beard and dark eyes that look soulless to me. "I bet Ricard would enjoy a taste of you. He likes his women tied up. It's easier for him to do the things he prefers to them, you see. Whenever I have a woman who needs to be tortured, I let Ricard do the honors. He enjoys it so much, you see, and it's a good reward, I think, for someone who is so loyal. Don't you think so?"

Rossi strokes my hair, which is sweaty and matted against my neck despite the cold. I jerk my head away, and he laughs.

"You should cooperate with me, Sofia. I can make your death easy, or hard. Has Luca ever told you why I have him be the one who tortures, more often than me, when we need information?" He smiles maliciously. "Oh, you can't respond, can you? Well, I'll assume that he hasn't. You see, Luca doesn't enjoy torture. Oh yes, your brutal husband, the one you're so afraid of, he's actually quite fussy when it comes to getting his hands dirty. Doesn't like to do it unless absolutely necessary. But that means he's *so* much more precise about it. Gets right to the point. But for me—" he breathes in as if savoring a sweet scent. "I love the screams, the blood, the pain. I love seeing them break, the moment when they realize that they can't take anymore and that they're going to tell me everything. The moment that they realize all the pain they endured was for nothing because they can't hold out. That they could have saved themselves so much, if they'd just talked right away. God, it's fucking delicious."

I shudder, feeling sick all over again. I haven't hated very many people in my life. I hated my father's nameless, faceless killers. I've thought that I hated Luca at times since I've known him, although I've also wondered often if that was just me fighting against the desire that I couldn't seem to stop. But I don't think I've ever hated anyone as much as I hate Rossi at this moment. Everything about him, from his thick sweaty hand running down my throat to his cold dark eyes to the sound of his voice, gloating about the pain he's caused so many other people, makes me sick to my stomach, burning with anger despite the cold that feels as if it's seeped down to my bones.

"Go ahead," Rossi says, nodding to Ricard. "Cut her clothes off."

There's no fucking way I'm making this easy for them. The minute Ricard reaches for my sneakered foot, I shove myself down the bed as hard as I can, driving my foot directly into his face. I don't get much of a kick in, but it's enough to push him back a little, a startled yelp coming from him as he raises his hand to his bleeding lip.

He's going to try to make me regret that; I know it. But I can't. Whatever they do to me, at least I drew first blood.

At least I tried to fight back.

I thrash on the bed again, trying anything I can to drag my hands free of the bindings, but I can't. It feels as if they get tighter. If anything, the circulation is slowly being cut off as my hands feel numb. One of the other men grabs my left foot as Ricard yanks my sneaker off of my right, and he squeezes my foot, running his thumb up and down the ball of it.

"I like your feet, *Bambina*," he says, his accent thickening. "Maybe I'll take a toenail or two to get you back for splitting my lip, and then I'll have you rub it over my dick until I get nice and hard for you."

I stare at him in horror. *How can someone even imagine something so awful?* The depravity of the man shocks me, and I have a feeling it's only going to get worse.

It would be easy to take my jeans off. My legs aren't bound. But this isn't about ease. It's about terrifying and humiliating me. "Don't squirm, baby," Ricard says, moving up the bed to straddle my thighs, the point of his knife shoving underneath the button of my jeans. "I don't want to cut that pretty skin of yours by accident." He grins, showing too-white teeth. "Every slice I make into you I want to enjoy."

Fuck. If he keeps this up, I *am* going to vomit. I try to spit the gag out again, but it's impossible. My eyes are watering as I try to hold still, every muscle and nerve in my body screaming to fight, to thrash, to try to get him off of me. It takes everything I have to deny that instinct, but the knife he's holding looks long and sharp, glinting in the overhead light of the room. The last thing I want is my guts sliced open by accident because this man is getting off on cutting my jeans off of me.

Ricard drags the knife downwards, cutting through the thin denim of my designer jeans—made for looks, not durability—all the way down the leg. I squeeze my eyes tightly shut when the knife slides over my inner thigh, telling myself that I won't think about Luca. I won't think about him kneeling between my legs on our wedding night, cutting into the soft flesh there with a knife like the one Ricard is holding, letting me bleed onto the sheet for a moment before bandaging it. I don't want to think about Luca's hand on my leg or the way that just minutes before, he was inside of me, kissing me as if he never wanted to stop as he lost control.

I don't want to think about any of that while a different man slides his hand down my leg, looking down lasciviously at me as he tosses my shredded jeans to the side.

Ricard looks disappointed as he sees my black cotton bikini panties, hooking his finger under the edge of the waist. "All that money and this is what you choose? I hope the pussy underneath is prettier than the wrapping."

"Leave her underwear on for now," Rossi orders. "Cut off her shirt."

"Yes, sir," Ricard says, but I can hear the disappointment in his voice. He squeezes my inner thigh, and I feel the pad of his finger trace the scar left from my wedding night. "Oh? What's this? Not the first man to put a knife between your thighs? What a little slut." He presses the knife against my left thigh, poking the point of it into my skin until my eyes water. "Maybe I'll give you one right here, to match."

"The shirt, Ricard." There's an anticipation in Rossi's voice that makes me feel sick all over again. He's old enough to be my father and then some, but here he is salivating as he watches his goon strip me. I glare at him, trying to put every ounce of hate and disgust I feel for him into my eyes as Ricard drags the tip of his knife down my breastbone, pressing the blade into the neckline of my thin t-shirt.

He cuts downwards a little and then grabs the shirt with one hand, ripping it down the middle so that my black bra is visible to everyone in the room. I cry out behind the gag, the sound muffled, doing my best not to let the tears burning behind my eyes fall. *Don't think of Luca*, I tell myself. He'd torn my shirt off too, stripped me naked partially against my will, but it hadn't been anything like this. Even his violence had been seductive and sensual, lust-filled in a way that aroused me despite myself, called to something deep and dark inside of me that I'd never recognized until him.

This is nothing like that. Ricard sneering down at me as he cuts the rest of my shirt away is light years away from Luca in every way. I wish more than anything that I didn't have this stupid gag in my mouth so I could spit in his leering face.

"Alright, that's enough for now," Rossi intones. He leans towards me, a cool smile on his face. "Now, Sofia, do you believe I'm serious?" He frowns. "Oh, you still can't talk. If I have one of my men take the gag out, will you promise not to scream?"

I nod, fully intending to shriek my brains out the minute the gag is out of my mouth. After all, what are they going to do, kill me? There's very little they can do to me that I don't think they already have planned. There's going to be torture probably, rape almost certainly, death definitely. They could make it worse, but to be completely honest, I'm not sure how it can get much worse. The sick anticipation of what they're going to do is rapidly becoming the worst part. If they'd just hurry up and do it, that would be better than this endless game-playing.

"Leo, take her gag out."

The man who approaches me is tall and lean, handsome in a young sort of way, and I wonder what Rossi has on him that's making him go along with this. He doesn't look as if he's particularly enjoying himself as he unbuckles the strap holding the gag in my mouth, his eyes carefully averted from my half-naked body. I make a note of him—if anyone is going to break at some point and help me out of this, it'll be him. But he doesn't really look like the hero type. If he was, he wouldn't be here in the first place.

I don't think there's going to be any kind of dramatic rescue, to tell the truth. I think I'm well and truly fucked.

The second the soggy mass of fabric is pulled out of my mouth, I do exactly the opposite of what I agreed to. My mouth feels dry and parched, but I draw the deepest breath I can. With every ounce of strength I have, I shriek so loudly that if there's anyone in the vicinity, I don't know how they could possibly *not* hear me.

"Help! Help me, please, please help me! Help, help, he—"

The blow comes out of nowhere, rocking my head to the side as pain blooms across my cheek and through my head, my jaw snapping shut and biting into my tongue. I taste blood, tears springing to my eyes, but I don't have a chance to collect myself before the same blow lands on the opposing side of my face, sending my head flinging to the other side.

I can feel blood trickling down my lip. I've never been hit before, and the pain is startling. I can't speak. It feels as if I can't breathe, the air knocked out of me with the shock, and my head lolls towards Rossi, my eyes a little unfocused as I look at him.

"Luca mentioned you were a little liar," Rossi says casually. "I thought he might have been exaggerating—you know, marital spats and all of that. But you really are a lying little bitch, aren't you?" He glances at Ricard. "You don't like women who lie, do you?"

"Nope. Not since my old lady stepped out on me and took my brother's cock up her ass." Ricard runs his finger over the edge of his knife blade, his eyes glittering at me. "I enjoy carving up lying cunts. Really gets me hard, hearing them beg for mercy."

His tone is conversational, as if he and Rossi are discussing the weather or where they ought to get lunch. I feel like I might burst into tears, and I struggle to hold it back. If I'm going to die, the last thing I want to do is die crying like a baby, begging for them to stop. Whatever they do to me, I'm going to do my best to take it and die cursing them, not pleading.

I'm sorry, I think to myself as Ricard grins at me, and Rossi leans back in his chair, clearly preparing to question me further. *I'm sorry, little baby. I'm sorry I couldn't protect you.*

I tried.

I really did.

LUCA

2

I'm still at my office when the alert goes off that tells me Sofia is no longer in the apartment.

That expensive diamond bracelet I gave her *was* because I wanted to do something nice for her. In a moment of what I suppose was weakness, I wanted to give her something beautiful. But it was a practical gift, too.

There's a tracker embedded in one of the daisies, linked to my phone to alert me if she leaves the penthouse. The problem is, I just so happened to step away from my phone the moment it goes off. By the time I get back to my desk and see the alert on my screen, the small dot on the map representing Sofia is at St. Patrick's Cathedral.

"Fuck!" I shout the word into the empty room, snatching up my phone and making a beeline for the door, texting my driver to meet me at the curb as I hurry towards the elevator. If he's not there by the time I get out to the street, I'm taking a cab, and I've never taken a cab in my entire life.

But I'm not wasting a single second getting to Sofia.

Why the fuck did she leave the penthouse? I rage internally, my blood boiling higher with every step I take. *Why can't she just fucking follow instructions for once in her goddamn life?* I'm sick to death of trying to keep her alive, of her fighting me every step of the way, driving me insane with her arguments and rebellion, and that fucking body that makes me hard just thinking about it.

There's no reason I can think of for her to go to the cathedral, but I'm sure she's got one—a stupid one, certainly, but a reason. *And I'm going to fucking love hearing it,* I think grimly.

If I have to guess, I'd say that she ran because of what I did last night, the way I fucked her with blood still on my shirt and used her like a mistress—not even that, really. A whore. I've never paid for sex, but I imagine that's about the way it goes. I fucked her like she meant nothing to me, and it was supposed to accomplish one thing—making her *believe* that she means nothing, so that she'd be afraid enough to listen to me and follow orders.

But clearly, it backfired and made her reckless enough to run instead. *What the fuck am I going to do with her?* I want to punch someone—not her, of course, I'd never lay a hand on her in any way other than sexually—but maybe one of the security guards, whoever was too busy refilling his coffee or jerking his dick to notice that my fucking *wife* was making a run for it. *I'm going to fire every single one of them,* I think angrily as the church comes into view. Better yet, I'll find out exactly who was on duty when Sofia went down in that elevator. I'll make sure he never sees anything ever again, since clearly, he has no use for his eyes.

It's still raining when I get out of the car, coming down in hard sheets that have left puddles by the curb, splashing up around my ankles, soaking the hem of my pants. I hardly notice as I take the steps up to the door of the church. My pulse speeds up with anticipation of danger when I see the door hanging open, the dim light from inside spilling out onto the steps. My hand automatically goes to the gun at my back, holding it in front of me as I step into the nave and slowly walk into the main aisle.

At first, I think it's empty, but then I see the hunched figure at the front of the pews. The blood on the floor, spattering the white floor grotesquely and dyeing the edge of the aisle runner a gritty brown.

"Father Donahue?" I call out his name as I walk carefully down, my gun still at the ready as I look around for anyone else who might still be lingering. "What happened here?"

The priest turns slowly, and I see the gash across the back of his head, still leaking blood. There's a purpling bruise on his forehead and the bridge of his nose, slowly spreading. By tomorrow he'll have at least one black eye.

"Someone got into the church," Father Donahue says quietly, and I can hear the shame in his voice. He stands slowly, taking careful steps towards me.

"No need to come to me, Father. You look like you might fall down at any second. *Who* got into the church?"

"I don't know," the priest admits. "I didn't see or hear them until they struck me. A blow across the back of the head, as you can see." His fingers gingerly touch the back of his neck, not daring to move up higher to the wound.

"You need to go to the hospital." I narrow my eyes at him. "I know Sofia was here. So tell me the truth, Father. Where is she?"

"I don't know," Father Donahue says, speaking quickly when he sees the look on my face. "It's the truth, Luca, by the Virgin Mother, I swear. When I woke up, Sofia was gone. Whoever broke in, they must have taken her." He looks at me carefully. "Is it the Bratva, do you think?"

"How the fuck would I know?" I snap. "They didn't speak at all? You didn't see or hear *anything*?"

"No."

"The Bratva are the most likely culprits." I rub one hand across my mouth, re-holstering my gun as I walk towards the priest. "Well, since you can't tell me anything about who kidnapped my wife, maybe you can tell me something else, *Father*." I take a menacing step towards him, feeling the rage bubble up in me again, hot and immediate. "Why did Sofia come to see you?"

"You know I can't tell you that, Luca." Father Donahue raises his hands, shaking his head as he takes a step back. "The seal of the confessional—"

"I don't give a good goddamn about the confessional." My lips press together, thinning into a tight line, and my hand itches for my gun. But even I wouldn't shoot a priest. I don't have much hope of heaven, but I'd prefer my particular circle of hell to not be too warm.

The temptation is there, though.

"Luca, I can't tell you. I *won't*," the priest says firmly. "You can do whatever you like, but I take my vows seriously and the sanctity of this place that you stand in. This church is a sanctuary, and Sofia came to me for just that. I won't break that confidence."

"Sanctuary from whom, exactly?"

Father Donahue gives me a sad look, and I can see the disappointment written across his face. Disappointment in *me*. It hurts more than it should, to be honest. There's a certain kind of low you have to reach to disappoint the priest who sprinkled water over your forehead while you squalled loudly enough to fill the entire church, who laid the first communion wafer on your tongue, heard you take your saint's name, took your first confession. The priest who heard you mumble your teenage failings from the other side of the screen, admitting to the tits you fondled and the ones you didn't but wanted to, the candy you stole even though you didn't need to, and the lies you told your parents. Those confessions always had to be dragged out of me. Even as a child, I was Luca Romano, raised to be *someone*. Raised to be wealthy, to be powerful, to never be told no.

To tell the truth, I think the man standing in front of me is the only one who ever has, and the only one who could ever get away with it.

That just pisses me off more, though.

"The man Sofia ran from isn't the man you are, Luca." Father Donahue sinks into the pew, his hands trembling slightly from his injuries. "I believe that. And I told her the same thing. But she came to me for help, and I had promised her father—"

"Her father extracted a lot of fucking promises," I snarl. "I'd have liked to know who Giovanni Ferretti was, that he has everyone doing his fucking bidding. Even me. *I* tried to keep Sofia safe. I married her, I bedded her, I gave her shelter and my protection. I saved her from Vitto, at risk to myself. And yet she still ran away from me."

"And why might that be, Luca?" Father Donahue's face is impassive, and another jolt of fury runs through me, making me see red.

"I'll give you one more chance, Father—"

My phone beeps then, alerting me that it's picked up the signal in Sofia's bracelet again. My pulse leaps in my throat as I zoom in on the blinking dot, moving across the map, and my blood runs cold all over again when I realize where that road is going. I know that route. I've been on it before. There's a safe house at the end of that road, one that I've secured in the past, taken shipments to, threatened men at.

It's one of Rossi's safe houses.

Rossi kidnapped Sofia.

My pulse roars in my ears, and I can feel the blood rising in my face, flushing me red as I clench my fist. "Thanks for nothing, Father," I manage through gritted teeth. "You should probably go to the hospital for that injury." I pause, glaring at him. "And this one."

I strike the priest hard with one well-placed swing, my fist connecting with his jaw and knocking him back. He tries to sit up, but I hit him once more, hard enough to knock him out so that he slumps to the floor out cold.

I shake my hand, wincing at the pain radiating from my knuckles. I shouldn't have done that; I know it, but I just couldn't help it.

It was far too satisfying. And besides, I'll call someone to take him to the hospital on my way out. Right before I go get my wife.

And kill everyone who dared think they could take her away from me.

SOFIA

3

"I'm not about to let you be the downfall of all I've built."

Rossi's voice cuts through the fog of pain. I blink at him, wanting to ask questions of my own, but I can't force them past my hoarse, ragged throat. I stopped screaming what feels like hours ago when I realized that no one could hear me.

No one is coming to save me.

No one ever was.

The torture Rossi devised for me is so much worse than I'd imagined. I'd pictured him yanking out my teeth one by one, ripping off my nails, burning the soles of my feet. The kinds of things you see in gangster movies. Instead, Rossi did something much worse.

He had Ricard inject me with some kind of drug, something that makes my veins feel like they're on fire from the inside. It made my brain foggy, my skin feels swollen and sensitive, so every touch is painful. I feel like I'm floating on a cloud in Hell, and I can only imagine that it's going to get worse.

Rossi has asked me all kinds of questions, ones that I don't have answers to. He asked me about Luca's business with the Russians, about his plans, about what he's talked with Viktor about. About whether or not he's going to war with them. The only thing I could tell him was that the last time I saw Luca, he was covered in someone else's blood. That seemed to please Rossi, and he told Ricard to stop touching me for a minute. Since the drug took hold, Ricard's hands have been on me for every second of it, running over my arms and breasts and stomach and thighs, not anything worse, not yet. I can't begin to imagine how awful that might feel because every time Ricard touches my skin, it feels like he's stroking raw flesh.

I've never felt anything as terrible as this, and it's not even over yet. I'm not at the point of begging for death, not quite, but every time I consider it, the same thought flits through my head.

My baby.

The thought of what the drug they injected me with might be doing to the baby makes my eyes fill with tears, tears that make Ricard chuckle and Rossi smile. Will, the young man who took my gag out, seems to be trying not to watch what they're doing to me. The other two men, whose names I haven't heard spoken—or maybe I have, and I just can't remember it through the fog of pain—watch but don't participate. Clearly, Ricard is Rossi's star torturer in all of this.

"The drug that we're giving you will kill you eventually, Sofia," Rossi continues. "I didn't want to tell you that until now because I'd hoped you'd give us more information. And if you know you'll die, well, there's not nearly as much incentive, to be honest, now is there? But maybe I can convince you to share in other ways."

He glances at Ricard, who rubs the front of his pants suggestively. I can see that he's hard, that he's getting off on this, and it makes me feel sick. I can taste bile at the back of my throat. I feel my stomach heave, a trickle of vomit slipping out of my mouth to join the rest of the fluids on my chin and cheeks, previous vomit and blood and saliva all mixed together.

Maybe I'm glad Luca isn't here to see me like this. I don't know why I care, but I do. I don't want his last memory to be of me half-naked on a bed, shuddering with pain and covered in my own bodily fluids. But then again, what will his last memory of me actually be?

Me on his bed, cringing away from him while he comes on my face, his angry eyes glaring down at me even in the middle of pleasure. Hardly a romantic way to leave things. But that was his choice, not mine.

Very little about our relationship was ever my choice. But for a little while, at least, I thought there was something there.

I think that hurts the most. How wrong I was. About Luca.

About us.

About everything.

"Cut off the rest of her clothes," Rossi orders coldly, and I squeeze my eyes shut tight, feeling tears trickling out of the corners. I just want this to end. I choke back a sob as I feel Ricard's cold blade cutting off my panties, and the words spill out that I've tried so hard to hold back this entire time.

"Please just kill me. Please, I just want it to stop. Kill me—"

Rossi laughs, but there's no humor in it. "Ah, there it is. I have to admit, you lasted longer than I thought you would. But it's not time yet, princess."

"What?" My head lolls towards him, and I'm momentarily distracted. "I'm not—"

"Sure you are." Rossi's eyes flick disinterestedly over my naked body as Ricard cuts away my bra, his hands skimming over my nipples as he pulls the cups away. It feels like hot needles stabbing into my skin, and I scream, although at this point, it's nothing but a whimper. "Luca's princess. Viktor's, if Luca hadn't rescued you." He leans closer. "Bratva princess. Mafia princess. They all want you. Luca, because deep down, saving you makes him feel like a better man than he is. Viktor because—well, that doesn't matter." He smiles at me. "Tell me, Sofia, what deal was Luca planning to make with Viktor?"

"I told you," I sob. "I don't know."

"So he never told you anything?" Ricard's voice cuts through the fog now, his fingers sliding up my inner thigh. "You're telling me this sweet pussy never got him to spill any secrets? Now that I don't believe."

"Tell us, Sofia," Rossi says, his voice darker now. "I've kept Ricard off of you for this long, but I won't keep him on the leash much longer if you don't talk. You'll die one way or the other, but you can die like you are now, or thrashing on the end of Ricard's dick. Imagine how much pain you feel now, but multiplied. Especially when I let the others at you, too." His voice slithers over me, and I'm reminded of the way Luca's voice would wrap itself around me when he seduced me, like smoke, like silk, like the first taste of expensive rich wine. Something that makes you feel sensual, dizzy, a little drunk. This is nothing like that, though. This slides over me like the scales of a snake, wrapping around me, strangling me with fear. I thought it couldn't get worse, but Rossi is right; he could make it so much worse. I don't want to die like that, violated by Rossi's henchmen.

I don't want to die at all.

And the worst part of it is that I don't know anything to tell. Even if I were willing to give up Luca's secrets to ease my pain, to tell Rossi everything, I literally *can't*. Luca never told me anything about his business with Viktor or anyone else that matters—probably for this exact reason, so that if his enemies ever got ahold of me, I wouldn't be able to tell.

I'm sure he never imagined that enemy would be his former boss, a man he looked up to like a father.

Worse yet, that attempt to keep me in the dark for my own safety is now just ensuring that my end is as horrible as it could possibly be.

"I don't know," I whisper helplessly. "I don't know anything."

It's the truth. But I know beyond a shadow of a doubt that nothing can save me now.

Not even that.

I feel the prick of a needle in my arm as Ricard injects more of the drug into my veins, and my heart sinks. *This is it,* I think dully, my head swimming. They'll keep me alive long enough to have their fun with me, and then they'll let me die.

My blood feels like it's boiling. My skin is feverish, itchy, tingling with a thousand tiny ant bites. I close my eyes, trying to rise above the waves of pain, trying to block it all out, trying to—

I think I hear sounds outside—the spitting of tires on gravel, the slamming of a door, a voice that I recognize shouting.

But it's all a dream. It must be the last grasping attempt of my mind to pretend that everything that's happening now isn't. That I'll make it out of this alive.

Just give in.

"Fuck, we gave her too much. Man, let me get in there before she dies—" Ricard's voice, thick with lust and making me want to gag.

"Just do it anyway. As long as she's warm, who cares?" Another voice, one of the men whose names I don't remember.

And then that shouting again, that voice that sounds so familiar. I want to drag myself up out of the depths, to respond to it, but I can't.

I'm sinking, and I'm grateful for it. At least I'm going to die now.

Before anything worse happens.

I'm sorry. I'm sorry.

LUCA

I HOPE I'M NOT TOO LATE.

The drive to the safe house was torturous. The minute I saw the address where the tracker stopped, I wasted no time getting back to my building and taking the fastest car I own, driving myself straight towards that blinking dot representing my wife.

I don't trust anyone else to get me here, and definitely not in one of the sleek cars that drive me around town. Normally the gleaming black Maserati is a car I'd take out on a pleasure drive. But there's nothing pleasurable about this trip, speeding along the freeway at a pace that ought to alert every cop in the Manhattan area. Fortunately, no lights show up in my rear-view. If they had, no cop who wanted to keep his job or ever work again, anywhere, would bother so much as lecturing me once he ran my plates and saw who the car belonged to. But I don't have time for that.

I know Rossi, and if he really is who has Sofia, and not someone gone rogue or some Russian who discovered the safe house, he isn't going to waste time. She's being hurt right now, if she's not already dead, and every cell in my body screams that whoever it is—Rossi or otherwise—will die screaming. Loyalty only goes so far.

No one touches what's mine.

It gets trickier once I reach the winding roads that lead deep into the woods upstate, where the safe house is located. It's dark, and the turns are sharp and tight. I try to exercise some caution—after all, I can't save Sofia if I wrap the Maserati around a tree—but it's almost impossible. I can hear my pulse thundering in my ears, my entire body consumed with an almost primal need to get to her. Visions of everything I've ever done to others swim in front of my eyes, now replaced with Sofia—with her screams, her blood, her pain.

Is this some kind of sick karmic joke? Some sort of punishment for everything I've inflicted on others?

This is exactly why I didn't want to get involved with her—with anyone. I grip the steering wheel so hard that my knuckles turn white. I *knew* this would happen at some point. If I dated someone, fell in love, or married, someone would take that person and use them against me. Hurt them to get to me.

I just hadn't expected it to be the man who I once considered the closest thing I had left to a father.

I'm not going to fucking let them get away with it.

It's possible, of course, that it's not him. But deep down, I know the truth. Rossi wasn't ready to hand the reins of power over. He wanted to do it in his own way, in his own time. He certainly didn't want to be relegated to the sidelines while I handled the conflict with Viktor in a way that he doesn't approve of. He'd thought he could continue to rule through me, and when I chose to put my foot down and use my new power—

I want to believe that Rossi would never do this. But I've seen too much of what he *is* willing to do to really think that.

The tires spit gravel as I pull up in front of the safe house, not bothering to disguise my arrival. I'm not sneaking in. Rossi has to know that I'd come for her, and doubtless, he has every entrance covered. I'm going in through the front door, and I'm going in guns blazing.

I stride towards the door, the gravel crunching under my leather shoes as I pull out the two P30Ls I've brought with me, the grips fitting in my palms too comfortably. I've rarely needed to shoot other men; more often, they die at the hands of our soldiers when I'm finished questioning them. But I've spent enough time at the range, preparing for a day like this, that my hands wrap around the pistols like they're old friends.

I hear a sound from inside, a ragged weak scream, and my blood boils over. I see red as I kick the door open, slamming my foot into it so hard that the edges splinter as it slams open, revealing the interior of the safe house.

"Where the fuck are you!" I shout, my voice echoing through the main room. I hear the noise again, a quieter whimper this time, and the sound of conversation coming from one of the back bedrooms. Without a second thought, I stride down the hall, my teeth gritted as I search for the room that has my wife.

When I kick open that door, my worst fears are confirmed. And the sight in front of me is more horrifying than I imagined.

Sofia is tied to the bed, completely naked, her face bruised and swollen. Though I don't see a hint of injury beyond the blood coming from the beating she clearly received, she's writhing on the bed as if she's in excruciating pain, her split and swollen lips parted as she whimpers. I've seen it dozens of times, that point where the throat hurts too much to scream, too battered and swollen, but the person doing the screaming still thinks they're shrieking when in fact, they're only mewling like a kitten.

Seeing her like that, knowing the point they've pushed her to, shoves me over the edge into madness.

Rossi is by the bed in his wheelchair, and he turns abruptly around, his face paling slightly as he sees me. *So he wasn't trying to lure me here.* I recognize Ricard, a member of Rossi's torture squad that I always despised and planned to get rid of as soon as the Bratva were dealt with. I had time to reassess the men I wanted to surround myself with. The others are just faceless soldiers to me, made men who no doubt have their own reasons for following Rossi into this madness. I don't care about them. They'll die, of course, but I don't give two shits why they're here or what their reasoning is.

I care about why the fuck Rossi decided to kidnap and torture my wife. And I want to know before I put him in the ground.

"You better not have let that filth rape her," I snarl, striding into the room with one P30L pointed at Ricard and the other at Rossi. "If he so much as touched her—"

"Oh, I fucking touched her." Ricard lifts his hand to his nose and sniffs dramatically. "Your wife's pussy is fucking sweet, *Principe*."

I don't even think about what to do next. I just react.

Ricard's screams fill the room as the first bullet goes directly into his knee.

"Anyone else have something smart to say?" I look around the room. The blond man's face has gone pale, and he looks like he might be sick. The other two look a little ashen as well, and they shake their heads.

"We were just following the don's orders—" one of them starts to say, and I fire again, his screams joining Ricard's as my shot hits him squarely in the shoulder.

"*I* am the fucking don," I growl out, my voice a low snarl. "You answer to *me*. And I promise you, you will answer for this with your lives."

"You're fucking weak is what you are," Rossi spits. "I should have killed Sofia from the start and never given you the option to marry her. I thought that letting you fulfill Marco's promise would let you entertain your fantasies of being the sort of man who rescues damsels in distress while I handled the Russian threat. I didn't expect to be forced to hand you the title so soon. Or for you to forget every fucking thing I ever taught you."

"You didn't teach me to torture and rape women."

"Don't worry, Ricard hasn't stuck more than his fingers in her. Yet."

A shudder of rage grips me, my vision darkening at the edges as I hold the gun steady, pointed at his face. "You would have forced *me* to do that, Vitto. Don't think I forget how you told me to take her virginity on our wedding night, one way or another. Luckily, she consented. But you would have had me killed for refusing to force my wife."

"She's your wife." Rossi waves a hand carelessly. "She belongs to you."

"Exactly." I grit my teeth. "So I'm taking her out of here and back home."

"No. I won't allow her to destroy this family and all that I've built. Sofia should have died years ago, along with her whore of a mother. I should have killed Giovanni and that Russian bitch before he ever got the chance to make a baby with her. I don't regret his death, Luca. I only regret that your father died avenging him. Marco was a good man, too good to die for a traitor like Giovanni Ferretti."

My next bullet goes into the blond man's head. I hear him drop, and Sofia lets out a squeal of pain or terror, I don't know. When I look over at her, I can see that her eyes look glazed, as if she's not really seeing me. I'm not even sure that she knows it's me here, right now.

"I've got plenty left," I say darkly. "So what's it going to be, Vitto? Do I let your remaining men live, and you, and take my wife home? Or are you going to continue to tell me how Sofia is a threat to the biggest crime syndicate in the world? You can't tell me one woman could bring all that down."

"Not all of it, no. But if Viktor gets his hands on her—"

"He *won't*," I snarl. "Viktor Andreyev will never touch my wife."

"You can't guarantee that. Especially not with this bullshit peace that you're insisting on." Rossi shakes his head, a disgusted look on his face. "You're weak, Luca. I should never have given you the title. Franco would have been a better choice."

"C'mon, boss, the girl is going to die before I get a crack at her if the *Principe* keeps talking—"

Ricard's body makes the most satisfying sound as it hits the floor.

"I can do this all day." I stare evenly at him, holding back the torrent of rage that makes me want to murder everyone in this room slowly, as slowly as I know how. "What happens if I let you walk out of here, Vitto?"

I can see him considering his answer. Surely he knows he's pushed me too far, that there's no coming back from this. Finally, with a deep sigh, he tells me the truth.

"I won't stop until she's dead, and every last Bratva dog is wiped from the face of this earth."

"That's what I thought." I raise the gun, and I hear two more cock behind me. "Don't bother," I say without turning around. "Your boss will be dead before you can pull the trigger, and my men will shred to you pieces for killing me. It's not worth it. At least I'll give you a quick death."

I hear the scrambling of their feet as they make a break for the back door. I turn swiftly, shooting them both in the back of their heads. They fall face down, and I hear the sound of the guards at the back making a break for it, no doubt knowing by now exactly who's found them. They might have been willing to back Rossi up against all intruders—but not me. I have the power of the rest of the organization behind me...and dedicated men who won't let them escape justice. Their best bet is to get a head start.

And I'm running out of time. I don't know what they did to Sofia, but she needs to get to a hospital. Soon.

"I'm sorry, Vitto." I turn back to him, and I see the old man's face pale as he realizes at last that no one is going to save him—that no one is going to stand up to me, choose him over me in the face of death. "You were like my father after my own died. You taught me a great deal that I'll always use and other things that I hope one day I'll be able to forget. But you've gone too far." I press the barrel of the gun against his forehead, and though my pulse is racing, my hand is steady.

There's no questioning my decision. But that doesn't make it easy.

Rossi's hand tightens around something in his fist. "Fine," he rasps, staring up at me defiantly. "Kill me. But ask Viktor when you see him. Ask him why he wants Sofia."

I look down at the man I once thought I loved like a father, and I feel nothing. Only rage turning from hot to cold in my veins, the world narrowing around me as I pull the trigger.

"I don't fucking care."

The shot rings in my ears. Rossi slumps forward, and as his body relaxes into death, his hand falls open, letting me see what he was holding there.

It's a cross necklace, edged in diamonds so minuscule I almost can't see them.

Sofia's necklace. The one she always used to wear that her mother gave her.

I'd wondered why she'd stopped wearing it. Now I know. Rossi stole it from her at some point—God only knows when.

I can feel the blood starting to rush through my veins again as I lower the gun, shoving them into their holsters beneath my jacket and at my back as I turn to the bed to grab her. She's cold to the touch, her breathing shallow and slow, and she's stopped writhing so much, although she's still twitching as if in pain. I wrap the blanket she's lying on around her body, cutting away the binding on her hands and lifting her into my arms. She feels light as a feather, and my chest constricts as I look down at her bruised face, blood and other fluids crusted on her lips and chin.

"I'm sorry," I whisper as I cradle her in my arms.

This is my fault. If I'd been colder, harder, more ruthless with her. If I'd made her fear me instead of making her start to love me. If I hadn't given her dates on rooftops and endless pleasure in bed. Maybe she would have been too terrified to ever leave the house.

I should have locked her in her room. Thrown away the key. Built a golden cage for her. Anything to keep her inside, away from men who would use her to hurt me.

You can never, ever give anyone reason again to believe that you care that much. Enough that she can be used as a weapon against you.

Not even her.

My mind is racing as I carry her out of the safe house to the waiting car. Her swollen eyes open for a moment, long enough to meet mine, and for a second, I think she might recognize me. Her lips start to form a word, but she can't speak.

"Shh. You'll be at a hospital soon, Sofia." I lay her in the backseat, careful not to jostle her. Still, it's clear that every touch and movement is excruciating. "I won't ever let anyone harm you again, my love." I don't touch her cheek, my fingers hovering over her face, and I let myself say the words just once. She won't remember them, after all. If she's lucky, her mind will block out as much of tonight as it's able.

"My love. My princess. My *queen*." I grit my teeth, taking in the sight of her lying there. "Everyone who did this to you is dead. And everyone who ever thinks about harming you will die. I promise, Sofia. I'll keep you safe from everyone."

Even me.

I get into the driver's seat, steeling myself for the drive to the hospital. When Sofia wakes up next, it'll be to the husband she remembers from the first days of our acquaintance. The one who is cold and hard, brutal and cruel, a man to be terrified of, a king to bow to, not one to love. It's the only way I can think of to keep her safe. I'll shun her in private, and if I'm ever able to take her out in public without fear of an attack, I'll be cold to her. I'll do everything I can to make sure that no one ever thinks again that kidnapping Sofia Romano is a way to get to me.

It's the only way I can think of to keep her safe. Even if it tears me apart.

SOFIA

5

*E*verything after that last injection is a blur. I think I went in and out of consciousness, although I remember clearly that the man who came into the room shot Will, the one who tried to be kind to me. I remember crying out at that, wishing that he hadn't had to die.

I wonder if they're all dead.

I wonder if Rossi's dead.

It feels as if someone's carrying me, wrapped in a blanket that feels like it's tearing my flesh off, but I'm too weak to scream or fight. I smell the leather of car seats, hear a voice murmuring above me as they lay me back on the cool surface.

My love. My princess. My queen.

I'll keep you safe from everyone.

My love.

It sounds like Luca's voice. But it can't be. Luca wouldn't say those things. He doesn't love me, or if he does, he loves me the way he might love a particularly beautiful piece of art. Something that belongs to him. Something that he bought that he can dispose of as he sees fit.

He doesn't love me like a woman. Like a *wife*. He proved that the last night I saw him.

The world fades out again, into a misery of fire, my body burning up from the inside. I have horrible visions of hands on me, hands I don't want, of my baby turning to ash in leaping flames as I try to grab for her, screaming the entire time as those hands drag me backward. I feel as if I'm floating, then drowning, and when I finally sink into unconsciousness, I can't help but hope that this is the death that Rossi promised me.

I can't bear any more of the pain.

* * *

THE NEXT TIME my eyes open, it's to glaring fluorescent light overhead. I still feel as if I'm floating, but it's in a kind of euphoria this time. There's no more pain. It's all washed away, and my body feels light. The absence of that pain in itself is a kind of pleasure, and I try to reach out to touch my belly, wondering if my baby is still there. If she survived. But I can't move. My hands won't move, I'm bound again, and I can feel myself thrashing, fighting, wanting to scream.

There are voices and hands. The prick of a needle, but this one doesn't bring pain.

Just more peace. More sleep. More rest.

Am I dead? Is this heaven?

* * *

I'M NOT DEAD, though. I find that out when I wake again, this time with more clarity. There's still the fluorescent lights and the feeling of euphoric painlessness. When I open my eyes, as dry and sticky as they are, I slowly become aware of my surroundings.

I'm in a hospital room, hooked up to machines, and my wrists are secured to the side of the bed with soft padded cuffs. There's a steady beeping, and I lick my lips, wishing desperately for some water. I'm about to try to get to the call button for a nurse when the door opens, and a short, dark-haired woman walks in in wrinkled scrubs, her eyes slightly lined.

"Mrs. Romano. I'm glad you're awake." There's palpable relief in her voice, and I wonder what happened since I passed out in the safe house that makes her look at me with that strange mixture of sympathy and concern. "Let me just undo your wrists."

"Why are those on there at all?" I croak. "Can I have some water, please?"

"Of course." The nurse undoes the cuffs, and I pull my wrists free, rubbing them even though there's no chafing from the cuffs themselves. They were soft and well padded, but my skin still feels irritated from the bindings that Rossi and his men tied me up with. "Here you go, Mrs. Romano." She hands me the cup, and the first touch of the cool water against my chapped lips feels better than the best sex I've ever had.

Well, maybe not that good. But almost.

I have to force myself not to gulp it down too fast. My throat feels parched, and I want to swallow it all at once, but I drink it in slow, measured sips instead that feel like torture, even now that I know what torture really is.

The memory of the fire in my veins makes me shudder, and the nurse looks at me with that same worried expression in her eyes.

"Why the cuffs?" I ask again when my mouth no longer feels sticky and dry.

"You were thrashing around too badly when your husband brought you in, scratching at your arms, out of your mind with pain. We had to restrain you so you wouldn't tear your own skin off." The nurse swallows hard. "I'm sorry this happened to you, Mrs. Romano. If you want to talk to someone—"

"No, that's okay," I say quickly. I have no idea what Luca's reaction to all of this will be, but I don't imagine weekly treks out to a therapist's office are in my future. Maybe if I could find one to do house calls—

He's never going to let me leave after this. I'm relieved to find out that the wrist restraints were the hospital's doing because, for a moment, I'd thought Luca had done it himself or ordered them to keep me from waking up and running away.

It hadn't even occurred to me when I'd first woken up, but now I wonder if there might be a chance between when the nurse leaves and when Luca comes to find me. "How long have I been asleep?"

"A few days," the nurse says. "Your husband has hardly left the hospital. He looked like a man possessed. He was so angry." She frowns. "We had to let him shower here, he refused to leave your side the first night to clean up, and he was—" she pauses, as if she's not sure how much to say. "Bloody."

I married a bloody man. I think of the spatters on his shirt and arms when he'd come home that night, someone else's blood, someone who had screamed and begged and writhed the way I had. Luca would say they deserved it, but Rossi would have said the same about me. *He must be dead now,* I think, shivering a little. I have a vague memory of Will falling with a hard *thud* when Luca shot him, of my cry of protest because he was the only one who offered me any kindness. I don't remember much else, and even that I'd thought might have been a dream, a hallucination of rescue.

My hand goes without thinking to my still-flat belly, and a cold rush of fear licks down my spine. "My baby—" it comes out as a whisper, but the nurse hears me anyway. I look at her with wide, frightened eyes, unsure if I want to ask the next question.

Once she answers it, she won't ever be able to take it back. The little secret I'd carried, the thing I was willing to risk my life for, the baby that I'd pictured in my head, promised to love and protect, will be gone forever once she confirms it. *I'm sorry.* How many times had I thought that as I was writhing in that bed, being burned up from the inside out by that drug? I'd tried to save my baby and failed anyway. And now Luca's wrath will be fierce, I'm sure.

I've been frightened of my husband before, but now I'm terrified to see him.

"Your baby is fine. We confirmed the pregnancy while we were treating you for the drugs in your system. You're very lucky, Mrs. Romano. The doctor had to do the scans a couple of times to be certain. He wasn't sure how a fetus so small managed to survive that trauma—you're not yet past the point when it's common to have a miscarriage over nothing."

"How far along am I?" My voice is hushed, my throat tightening. *My baby is alive.* It feels impossible. I'd resigned myself some time amid all that torture that I was going to lose my child, that there was no way out of it. That we were both going to die. And yet here we both are, in a hospital bed, alive.

For now.

"Six weeks," the nurse says, with the first smile that I've seen on her face. "It's a very new pregnancy. You're very fortunate, Mrs. Romano, that either of you is alive."

"I know," I whisper. I've never been so sure of anything. And now that I've had that good fortune, I have to figure out what to do next.

My baby and I survived Rossi. But now we have to survive Luca.

My husband.

I still haven't gotten used to hearing his last name attached to mine.

"Does my husband know about the baby?" I can feel panic starting to claw at my throat, closing it even more. If Luca knows already, there's nothing I can do except maybe try to get out of the hospital before he comes to take me home. But even if I can manage an escape from here, I have no idea what I'll do next. I'm in a hospital gown, with no clothes here, no money, and nowhere to go. I can't put Ana in danger by going to her, and I'm not even sure if Father Donahue is still alive.

I'm even more trapped than I was before.

"Not if you haven't told him," the nurse says, looking at me curiously. "We haven't updated your medical file yet, and we thought it might be better to wait to say anything until we knew if you had or not. We didn't want to be the ones to spoil your surprise if—"

She stopped herself, but I knew what she was going to say. *If you both survived.*

Well, we did, and now I have to figure out what to do next.

This nurse is the only one who might be able to help me.

"I need you to leave it out of my medical file." I try to make my voice as authoritative as possible, but it's hard when it still feels raw from all the screaming I did. "I don't want my husband to know. Not right now."

She looks at me curiously. "I'm not sure if that's something I can do," she says carefully. "Leaving out medical information is—"

"It's important," I say, trying to keep the desperation out of my voice, but I can hear it creeping in. "It's—essential that he not know."

"You'll need to give me a little more detail than that." The nurse frowns. "Are you in some kind of danger? Do you need me to call someone? Maybe you'd like to talk to someone about your husband?"

I laugh at that. I can't help it, and it comes out as a sort of high-pitched, almost hysterical sound. The idea of anyone doing anything to Luca, protecting me from him, is too ridiculous. I try to picture myself talking to the police, filing charges against my husband for—what? A marriage I agreed to? Sex that I begged for? Luca's probably committed a hundred crimes, but he'll never see the inside of a jail cell. And to tell the truth, I'm safer with him than I probably would be anywhere else. Rossi would never have gotten his hands on me if I hadn't left the penthouse, a point that I expect my husband will drive home with great emphasis.

No matter how hard I try, I can't stop laughing until my arms are wrapped around my sore ribs, choking and gasping as I try to breathe through it.

The nurse looks understandably alarmed. "Mrs. Romano, do you need a sedative? I can—"

"No!" I shake my head, trying to collect myself. "I just—do you know who my husband is?"

"Luca Romano." The nurse looks a little confused. "I'm sorry, I'm new here. Is he a major donor to the hospital or something?"

Somehow, I manage to not start laughing again. "I'm sure he's made donations," I say as calmly as I can manage. "But that's not what I mean. My husband is the don of the American branch of the Italian mafia. And I'm sure if you ask whoever is in charge here, they'll tell you exactly what kind of man he is."

The nurse's eyes go wide. "I'm sorry," she stutters. "I've heard about—but I heard a man named Rossi—"

Just the sound of his name makes my stomach turn over. "I'm going to be sick," I manage just in time for the nurse to hand me a plastic container. I heave into it until my vision darkens at the corners and my throat burns all over again. There's nothing in my stomach to throw up, but my body does its best, bile spilling out of my mouth until there's nothing left of that, either.

When I'm finished, she takes it away and returns with that same worried look on her face. "Tell me what's going on," she says calmly. "And I'll see what I can do."

I'm not stupid enough to tell her everything. Just what I need to, to get her to go along with what I need.

"There's a clause in my prenup that says I can't get pregnant. If I do, then I have to terminate."

A look of horror spreads over the nurse's face. "What? Why on earth—"

"It's complicated."

"Why don't you just leave? Get a divorce—I'm sorry," she says abruptly. "I know it's not always so simple. But if your husband would—"

"I tried to leave," I say simply. "You see what happened."

"Your husband did this?" She goes white as a sheet. "Mrs. Romano, what was done to you—"

"No! No, Luca didn't do this," I say quickly. "But he's protecting me from people who would do this and much worse. I tried to leave because of my baby, and I was kidnapped. I can't just leave again. It's just out of the frying pan and into the fire. I have to figure out a different plan. But I need time." I look at her pleadingly. "I need to be able to tell him about this in my own time." *Or never. That would be better, if I can find a way out. But I just need time.* "If he sees my medical records, then I won't be able to figure out the best way to handle it first. I need some time."

The nurse lets out a long breath. "Alright," she says finally. "But Mrs. Romano—"

"Don't," I say quietly. "Whatever you're about to say, I promise it's more complicated than you realize. I'm not just some battered woman. My husband hasn't abused me. He's just—a difficult man." *That's putting it lightly.* "And I need to figure out what to do on my own."

"I'll make sure that your files don't make any mention of the pregnancy. And I'll suggest to the doctor that perhaps he was mistaken." She hesitates. "I can't promise that everyone who is aware will keep quiet. But I'll do all I can to keep it quiet."

I feel a rush of relief, the first I've felt in longer than I can remember now. "Thank you," I whisper, and the nurse gives me a small smile.

"You need to get some rest, Mrs. Romano. Your body has been through a lot. You need time to heal before you can go home."

That can take as long as possible, I think grimly. The last thing I want to do is go back to the penthouse with Luca. I'd stay awake forever if it could keep me here, in the relative safety of the hospital, instead of going back into my gilded cage. I shudder to think how furious he must be.

But the hospital can't protect me from Viktor and the Bratva. Even if Rossi is dead, he wasn't the only threat out there.

Luca has me caged for a reason; even I can't help but see that now. But my secret changes everything.

The nurse injects something into my IV before I can say anything. A shudder goes through me, remembering Ricard sliding the needle into my arm and the excruciating pain that followed. *How long will it be until I stop being reminded of that?* I wonder, and deep down, I know that it will be a very long time.

Maybe forever.

It's terrifying to imagine how long something like this will haunt me.

What do I do next? I have no idea if Father Donahue is alive, and I can't put him at risk again. Luca will expect me to go back there.

If Viktor wants me so badly, what would he be willing to do to get me? There's some reason why he wants me in his possession, why the

Bratva has nearly started a war over it. And whatever that reason is, I have a Russian mother. It's possible that I could somehow negotiate protection from the other side, something that they want in exchange for them making sure that my baby is safe.

It's a long shot, and I know there's probably not a chance in hell that it would work. If Luca is a beast, Viktor Andreyev is a monster. A wolf and a bear, respectively. But still—I can't shake the thought that there might be something there, some leverage that I can use.

I wonder if Ana might be able to find out something, somehow. *I'll ask her,* I think tiredly. *Once I get out of here.*

Whenever that might be.

I can feel the sedative taking hold, no matter how hard I fight it. My body craves rest, sleep, time to recover. And I can't fight it.

I slip away into a blissful, dreamless sleep.

LUCA

6

The hardest thing I've ever had to do is look Caterina in the eye after she heard the news of her father's death.

I don't regret killing Rossi. Once the doctors filled me in on the extent of what he and his thugs had done to Sofia, any trace of regret was entirely wiped away, if there had been any left after what I'd seen. It's impossible to wish that I hadn't killed him after holding Sofia writhing in my arms while that drug worked its way through her veins. Whatever leftover feeling I have for him, for all our history and everything he did for me after my own father died, was superseded by the knowledge of what he'd done to my wife.

And in the end, I suppose that's part of what he was afraid of all along when I said I wanted to marry Sofia rather than letting him simply eliminate her. That my loyalty to my wife would win out over all the other loyalties I might have held.

I'm still loyal to the family, to the title that I hold, and to the position I've been entrusted with. But in all my time underneath Rossi, I've never killed a woman. I know that Ricard was his choice for the occasions when he needed information from one, and I hated that. I hated that Rossi ever allowed it. And now that he and Ricard are both dead, I'll make certain that it will never happen again.

This family will be ruled by me, in my way. Nothing is stopping me from that now.

But it still hurts to see the pain written across Caterina's face.

Franco isn't here, which irritates me. He's been noticeably absent during all of his wife's crises, and I haven't forgotten it. I'm sure there are many men under me who aren't model husbands, but it's particularly irksome with Franco. He was given a wife far above what he should have expected, the daughter of the former don, and his behavior towards her is verging on disrespect—not just towards her but also her deceased father and me, for our decision to make the match.

I shake my head, shoving the thought away for now. At the moment, I have something more pressing than my best friend and underboss's refusal to leave his bachelor ways behind, and that's comforting the daughter of the man I just killed—and making certain that there's no suspicion that it was my hand that dealt the killing blow.

"You said it was the Bratva?" Caterina wipes her hand across her nose, sniffling. She's the least composed that I've ever seen her, and I can see that she's lost weight since her mother's death and her wedding. Her cheeks look gaunt, and she's very pale. Her hair, normally luscious and shiny and thick, something I always took note of even though I knew she was never meant for me, is pulled back in a bun and looks frizzy around the edges. "They killed my father?"

"And kidnapped Sofia," I confirm. "Your father, some of his men, and I went to rescue her, but the Bratva gunned them down."

"And how did you make it out, then?" Caterina frowns at me, her lips thinning. "That's awfully lucky."

I don't hear suspicion in her voice—I'm not sure anyone really *would* suspect me of killing Rossi. After all, if they don't know that he kidnapped my wife, I have no reason to. I already have the title. But I can see the confusion written plainly across Sofia's face.

"I was behind them in another car," I say quietly. "I'm sorry, Caterina. I got there too late. But I took several of the Bratva with me. A few others escaped, but the one who killed your father is dead. I shot him myself."

There it is. Neat, tidy. Any possible witness is already dead.

"Did he suffer?" Her chin quivers and I can tell that she's trying not to burst into tears again.

"No," I tell her firmly, and I'm glad that I can at least be honest about that. "It was quick."

"Are you sure? How—" a small sob escapes her, and I sink down to sit next to her.

"Do you really want to know, Caterina? You're torturing yourself here—"

I wince even as I say the word. I'm not sure I'll ever be able to think of torture so blandly again, as just a part of my job, a means of getting men to talk. I wonder how long it will be until I don't see Sofia's twisting naked body in front of my eyes, wracked with pain from the inside out. My fist clenches at my side, and I know in that second that if I could, I'd kill all of them, all over again.

"I want to know," she says firmly, lifting her delicate chin. "It'll be worse if I imagine it."

"He was shot in the head," I tell her as bluntly as I can, wincing as the words come out of my mouth. "He died instantly, Caterina. There's no other way that it happened."

She pales at that, but her chin stays lifted. "It's good that it was quick," she says finally. "I'll handle the funeral arrangements. I know he has a Will with his wishes outlined."

His Will has a great deal more than that for Caterina, I know. As his only child, she'll inherit the Rossi mansion, which I'm sure Franco will be thrilled to move into. She'll also inherit her father's vast wealth, the part of it that's separate from the family business. But I can see from looking at her face that she doesn't care about any of that.

Rossi deserved to die for what he did. But I know what an incalculable loss this is for her—her mother and her father, killed within weeks of each other. I can see the burden on her slender shoulders, and I wish that she had a better husband to help bear it for her. Franco has always been a good friend to me and a good man in so many ways. But in this, he's failing.

"Let me know if you need anything. I mean that, Caterina. Anything at all. Sofia—"

"I'm sure Sofia will need to rest. She's been through a lot." Caterina rubs her hands over her jean-clad knees, letting out a long breath.

"She'll want to help, though, if she can." Even I can hear the terseness in my voice when I talk about her. I might have torn through a house full of men to save her, but I'm still furious with her for leaving at all. I'll wait until she's well enough to bear the brunt of my anger, but there's going to be hell to pay when I get her home.

Caterina is quiet for a long moment. "So what now, Luca? You go to war with Viktor? All of your attempts to make peace are over, I guess."

I pause. "Well, that's at least partially up to you."

She blinks. "Me?" The confusion on her face is plain, and I can understand why. The mafia has never been much for taking the opinions of their women into account. But it matters to me what she wants. Even if it wasn't really the Bratva who killed Rossi—in a way, all this has come to pass because of them. And if Caterina wants someone to bleed for her father's death, I'm willing to take it out of their skins.

There's a stretch of silence between the two of us, and I can see her seriously considering her answer. Her eyes shimmer with tears, but they don't fall this time as she turns to look at me. "No," she says finally, her voice trembling but firm. "No, I don't want more death on top of all of this. You said the men who did this are dead. So that's enough."

A chill runs through me at that. The man who is responsible isn't dead, of course. He's sitting right in front of her. I wonder what she would say if she knew what her father had done before his death, the way he'd tormented her best friend, wracked her body with pain, and let one of his men assault her. The doctor assured me that Sofia wasn't actually raped, but I know it was a close thing if not. Ricard would have had his filthy hands all over her.

I wish I could have taken longer to kill him, in particular.

The lies about who was responsible for Sofia's kidnapping and Rossi's death weren't just to protect me. It was also to protect Caterina from having to know what her father did, what he was truly capable of. I want her to be able to keep her memories of him without them being tainted.

"Then I'll keep trying to make peace with Viktor." I wait for her to stand up, and then I do, too, my mind already drifting to Sofia. "I don't know if it will work. But I'll do all I can."

"I know you will," she says softly. "You're a good man, Luca." She pauses then as if wondering whether or not to say more.

"I want peace just like you do," Caterina continues. "Because Franco and I are trying for a baby. We decided not to wait. I could already be pregnant, and I—" her voice breaks off. "I don't want my child to be raised in a family full of blood and death and fear. I want this war to be over before then and peace on all sides. I know that's not what my father wanted. But in that respect, I'm not my father's daughter, and you Luca—you're not anything like him. I know you can make it happen."

"I'll try my best," I assure her. "You're right that this has gone on too long. I'll get to the bottom of it and find a way to bring this to an end."

"And—" Caterina hesitates. "Be patient with Franco, Luca. He's been—different lately."

I frown. "Different how?" I've seen it too, but I'm curious what she means by that.

"He's more impatient. Short-tempered…maybe a little paranoid, even. I think he's worried that the attempts to make peace will come back to blow up in our—your—faces. He's—" she spreads her hands helplessly as if she can't think of the right word. "Paranoid. That's the best I can come up with, really. And he's short with me in particular."

There's the sound of footsteps in the hall behind us, and I turn around. "Speak of the devil," I say with a short laugh. "Franco, it took you long enough to get here."

At the mention of his name, I see Caterina flinch, and I frown heavily, watching her as her husband approaches. There's a nervous expression on her face that worries me and makes me wonder if Franco's short temper has gone past just snapping at his wife or neglecting her. I'm not in the habit of monitoring the marital habits of the men underneath me, but I would never tolerate domestic violence from any of them. Rossi, ironically enough, didn't either—I remember a few occasions when wives came to him, battered beyond their ability to bear it, to ask him to step in. And he always did. Once the husband refused to change his ways, that woman became a widow, the husband a victim of an "accident."

It's always been an unspoken rule that mafia women who have abusive husbands don't go to the police. They go to the don. Going to the cops is equally unforgivable. And I intend to continue that. I'll never tolerate a husband abusing his wife. If Franco is doing that to Caterina, it's even less tolerable.

My eyes sweep over her quickly, looking for any visible bruises, but there's nothing that I can see. I hope that means that Franco hasn't been rough with her, but I make a mental note to keep a better eye on him. Whatever is bothering him, he needs to pull it together. I need my underboss to be on top of his game, not distracted and paranoid.

"I heard what happened," Franco says, dropping a quick kiss on his wife's cheek. "Is Sofia alright?"

"She's recovering. I was just talking with Caterina about our next steps with the Bratva."

Franco's eyes narrow. "Why? I didn't know we were in the habit of taking advice from women." His tone is joking, but I can see Caterina's expression darken.

"She's Rossi's daughter," I remind him. "She has as much say in what we do next as anyone."

From the look on his face, I can tell that Franco disagrees, but before he can say anything else, Caterina gives him a tight smile.

"I'm going to check on Sofia," she says, her tone falsely bright. "If either of you needs to talk to me about anything, you can find me there."

Franco watches her leave, his gaze raking over her backside as she heads down the hall. "She's losing weight," he complains. "That ass isn't what it used to be."

I glare at him. "She's lost both her parents in a matter of weeks, Franco. Give the woman a break."

He shrugs. "Hey, it's not like I can't find a plump ass somewhere else. Just saying, she's already letting herself go."

Inwardly, his attitude makes me seethe, but I push it aside. I'm not here to tell Franco to stop being a pig when it comes to his wife and women in general—and after all, it's not like I haven't had similar attitudes through the years. My inability to want any woman other than one has been a very—recent development.

Want hardly seems like a strong enough word for the desire I feel for Sofia. *Obsession. Addiction.* A savage need that tears through me at the most inopportune moments. Even now, I can feel that familiar ache for her, and I want to get her home.

I tell myself it's just so that she'll be safe, so that I can lock her away and turn my thoughts back to more important things. But I know that's not entirely the truth.

I want to punish her. Possess her. Make her mine again. Fuck her until every trace of the men who touched my wife, my property without permission, is wiped away.

I'm done catering to her sensibilities. She put herself in danger, and it's my job to make certain that never happens again.

As her husband. Her don. Her *master*.

"So—the plan?" Franco's voice cuts through my thoughts, and I turn my attention back to him and away from my errant wife and rapidly swelling cock. "What are we doing about those Bratva fucks?"

"Nothing," I say flatly. "I still want to make peace with Viktor, and Caterina has said the same. She doesn't want more blood in recompense for her father's death."

Franco stares at me, his eyes widening. "So you're going to do *nothing*? Your wife was just taken, my wife's father murdered—"

"I didn't say that I would do nothing," I cut him off, my tone harder than usual. "I'm going to call a meeting of all the bosses—a conclave. We'll work this out among ourselves, Italians, Russian and Irish, with everyone who needs to be in attendance. We'll settle this once and for all, without war, without more bloodshed."

"You should be asking for the Irish to stand at your side against the Russians," Franco argues hotly, his voice rising. "Colin Macgregor will stand with you, and you know it. You could wipe the Bratva threat off of the map and give their territory to the Macgregors."

"The fighting needs to stop," I say flatly. "Us not being able to come to terms has put Sofia in more danger—do you really think they'll stop at this? I need to find out what Viktor will accept to make peace. And you should be just as worried for Caterina. She could be a target as well." She *is*, from what Viktor told me, but I haven't shared that with Franco. I know that I should share with him that the Bratva *Pakhan* wants his wife as a prize, but lately, I haven't been so certain that I can trust his decision-making. And he's pushed against *my* decisions far too often recently, on top of that. "Aren't you worried about what damage a war might do to your family?"

"I'm more worried about the greater Family than just my wife," Franco snaps. "I'm a mafia man, just like you are, Luca. But you're so caught up in your own personal drama that you can't focus on the problem at hand here. You're putting your wife over—"

"Enough!" My voice is harsh and angry, more so than it's ever been with him, but I can't seem to stop myself. I feel brittle and furious, pushed to the brink by my wife's disloyalty, my best friend's erratic behavior, and the fact that not only did I just murder the closest person to a father that I had, but have to orchestrate covering it up as well. "I will not have war, Franco. Not if I can prevent it."

"The Irish—"

"Will attend the conclave, like the Russians and us if they know what's good for them, and we'll stay there until we can come to an agreement that all the families are pleased with. And then we will keep the peace that's agreed to." I narrow my eyes as Franco opens his mouth to argue again, my blood heating with righteous anger. It feels good to direct all that fury somewhere, all the pent-up rage that's been simmering since I pulled Sofia out of the safe house. "You'd do well to be cautious about your loyalties to the Irish, too. Someone with as many rumors surrounding him as you have ought to be careful in your arguments for them."

Franco's face is stunned as he stares at me, his mouth mercifully shut by that last comment. In all our years of friendship, I've never once thrown the rumors about his parentage in his face. It was always me who protected him from them. But at this moment, I'm past caring. I'm past all of it. Since I took the role of don, he hasn't been there as I'd hoped he would be. And I'm starting to grow tired of it not being reciprocated.

"I need to see to my wife," I say coldly, all of my patience runs dry. "You should see to yours."

And with that, I stalk off down the hall towards Sofia's room.

SOFIA

7

I don't know how long it is before I'm released from the hospital. Time stops having any meaning—it's no longer day or night, or hours in the day, but the spaces between consciousness, between being aware and sliding back into the healing rest that everyone is so insistent that I need. It would be more restful if the sleep were dreamless, but it's not.

My sleep is full of nightmares, of Ricard's leering face and Rossi's smirking one, of hands in places I don't want them and men looming over me, of burning fire in my veins. Worse still, the sedatives they give me don't allow me to easily wake up, so I'm left to fight my way through the bad dreams, all the way to the other side of it.

I wake once, hazily, to see Caterina at my bedside, but I'm not aware enough to actually acknowledge her. I wish I were because she's the only one I know for sure who came to see me. If Luca did, it's never been while I'm awake.

And I wouldn't be surprised if he didn't. I tell myself over and over that I don't care, hardening my heart against him with each day that passes so that when I finally end up back in the penthouse, I have armor to guard myself with. I tell myself that I won't play his games anymore, that I'll just go cold.

I'm not entirely sure I believe that. But it helps me get through the waking moments until the day that I'm finally cleared to go home.

Luca comes to get me. I shudder a little when I see him, the memory of him laying me in the backseat of the car still too fresh. That, combined with the knowledge of how angry he must be with me, makes me wish more than ever that I could just stay in the hospital.

"It's time to go home," Luca says with a thin smile, underscoring my anxiety. "Are you ready, Sofia?"

I'm as ready as I'll ever be. Someone left clothes for me—him or Caterina, I have no idea—and I'm already showered and dressed, feeling the most human I have since before I was knocked out at the cathedral.

Unbidden, my hand almost floats to my stomach before I can stop it, wanting to touch the secret I have there to protect it. But I manage to pull it back just in time, and if Luca notices anything about the motion, he doesn't say so.

We're silent all the way down to the curb where the car is parked. I'm not sure how Luca managed to get them to let me walk out under my own power, but I'm glad not to be wheeled out front. I've felt weak for too long, and it feels good to be standing on my own two feet again. Even if I know another storm is coming.

Sure enough, the moment that we're both in the car with the doors shut, the divider goes up that separates us from the driver and pulling into traffic, Luca rounds on me, his expression as cold and hard as I've ever seen it.

"What," he grinds out through clenched teeth, "the *fuck* were you thinking? Leaving like that? Going to St. Patrick's? What the fuck were you doing, Sofia?"

I could tell him the truth. It occurred to me for just a single moment that I could do that. I could put my faith in this man who has saved me more than once, who married me, who has despite his mercurial temper and predilection for rough sex has shown me that there's a side of him that does care for me—or at least did, until that last episode in our—*his*—bedroom.

It's that memory, more than anything else, that supersedes any others. That overrides any trust or faith I might have ever had in him. I've seen how quickly he can go back to his old self, the self that terrified me when we first met. And I can't trust that he'll break our contract to protect our baby.

I envision him telling the driver to turn the car around, to take me back to the hospital. Forcing me to terminate the pregnancy against my will. I remember the padded cuffs around my wrists, holding me down for my own good, and I know they could be used against me just as easily as the ones in the safe house were.

I might be kept safe, in his custody. But my baby isn't.

Lifting my chin, I look him straight in the eye, not flinching at the coldness of his green gaze. "I left because I'm done with all of this," I tell him, my voice sharp and cutting, like the lash of a whip. *See, I can do this too.* "I'm done with your lies, Luca, done with you breaking your promises, done with this fucking sham of a marriage. I'm done with you using me. So yes, I ran away. I went to see if Father Donahue would help me escape you. Because you've broken all of the promises you made me. I'm not safe. What happened just proved that."

"You were kidnapped because you ran away," Luca snaps. "If you'd stayed put like you were fucking told—"

"I don't care." I clench my teeth, and I'm not entirely sure that everything I'm saying is, in fact, a lie. "I thought there could be something between us when you flew back from the Dominican Republic that night. I thought we might be able to have something real. The dates, the way we were together for a little while—" I take a deep breath, still staring him down, even though my heart feels like it might beat out of my chest. "But I saw the other night when you came home bloody and did—what you did—I saw that it was every bit as fake as our marriage. We never had a chance, Luca. And I'm done pretending."

"What did I do?" Luca smiles coldly at me. "I came home bloody from trying to find out who attempted to fucking *kill* you. And after that?"

"You assaulted me—"

"No, I fucking didn't. Accuse me of whatever you like, but don't ever fucking accuse me of that. You wanted it. You were fucking soaking wet when I got my cock in you. Just like I bet you are now." He sneers at me, his eyes glittering with a dangerous anger. "I bet if I slid my hand up your thigh, you'd be dripping. You get off on this, on the fighting, the danger of it. On setting me off and seeing how far you can push me. One day, Sofia, you're going to push me too fucking far."

"And what?" I glare at him. "You'll tie me up and torture me like Rossi did?"

"Don't fucking say that!" His hand lashes out, grabbing my chin. "The driver might hear you."

"So what? Doesn't everyone know?"

"No," Luca grinds out through gritted teeth. "Because I had to fucking lie to cover up the fact that I killed him to get you out of there? Do you know what could happen to me—to you too—if the rest of the underbosses and capos found out what I did?"

"But—" I struggle in his grasp. "He was torturing me. He was going to let Ricard rape me. He was going to kill me—"

"Sure. And if I could prove that, then Rossi would have been executed after a trial in front of the council. But I went in there, guns blazing, vigilante-style. I killed them all to get you out of there because by the time I managed to take him and the others into custody, if my men and I survived that, you would have been dead. And in doing so, I risked *everything*, Sofia! Do you fucking understand that? Once again, I've laid everything on the line for you, and you, you—"

He trails off, fairly shaking with rage. "You are my *wife*," he snarls. "Call it a sham marriage if you want, call it all fake and lies and broken promises, but in the eyes of man and God and most importantly the fucking bosses of all the families, you are my legal and rightful wife. And just as you swore in front of that traitorous priest, by God, Sofia, you will fucking obey me if it's the last thing you do."

"Or what?" I know I shouldn't bait him, that he's already so close to snapping. But he's pushing my buttons, too. He's made me angry because I don't *want* to obey him. I never have.

I wanted the husband that I got a brief glimpse of. But that was a fucking lie, just like everything else.

"Goddamn it, Sofia!" Luca rakes his fingers through his hair. "Just —every single person in the mafia, from the highest underboss to the lowest soldier, fucking obeys me. Without question, without a word to my face. Maybe they bitch about my orders later; who fucking knows. But they *obey*. And I want, no, I *demand* that from you. Your obedience. Not your love, not your happiness, not your pleasure. Your fucking obedience. You do as I say and go where I say and fuck when I say. And then maybe we can both have some peace."

"You can't force me to fuck you if I say I don't want you." I cross my arms under my breasts, glaring at him. "Then you'd be doing the one thing you swear you won't do. And Rossi isn't here anymore for you to blame it on, to say he's making you."

Luca's expression changes in an instant, faster than I've ever seen it. His eyes warm, the anger replaced with the heated lust that I recognize so well. It's a startling change, but I know him well enough by now to know that it was always simmering under the surface, waiting for a reason to emerge.

His hand goes to my knee, sliding up past the curve of it. "You don't want me, Sofia?" His fingers slide up higher to the soft skin on my inner thigh. The place that he's touched so many times now, licked, kissed, nipped in the heat of passion. His fingers press in, and I stifle a soft gasp.

"No," I whisper, but it doesn't sound convincing. I clear my throat. "No." It sounds better the second time, and Luca's fingers go still, but his hand stays inside my skirt, his palm resting against the warm flesh.

"So if I slid these fingers under your panties, you wouldn't be wet for me?" His voice ripples over my skin, smoky and seductive, and I repress a shiver. I can already feel myself getting aroused, my folds slick and damp with it, and if he follows through on his threat, he'll know just how much I want him. That no matter how angry I am with him, how much I want to be cold, to reject him, my body says otherwise.

Because my body remembers exactly what he can do to it. What it can feel like when I give in.

Luca smiles at me, but it doesn't quite reach his eyes. "Answer me, wife."

"No." I swallow hard. "I'm not."

"You're not what?" His lips part, showing perfectly white teeth. *He's enjoying this.* He loves toying with me, like a cat with its prey.

Prey that wants to be eaten. To be devoured. To be…

"Oh!" I gasp as his hand slides higher, towards the heat between my legs, the damp gusset of my panties. "Luca, no!"

"You're not what?" He looks at me with that dangerous edge to his smile. "You know how I feel about being lied to. So tell me, Sofia. If I slide my hand higher, will I find out that you're wet for me?"

I know better than to lie to him. I've made that mistake before. But I can't bring myself to admit it. Not now. Not here.

Not like this.

"No," I whisper. That word keeps slipping from my lips, but it means nothing. "I'm not."

Luca's smile spreads, and I know then that he wanted me to lie, even though he'll punish me for it. "Oh, Sofia," he murmurs. "You should know better."

His fingers slide up then, up, up, under the edge of my black lace panties. Not what I would have chosen to wear home from the hospital, but they were all there was with my clothes. It makes me think Luca was the one who brought the clothes for me. They dip beneath the lace, stroking over the swollen folds of my skin, and I can't suppress the gasp that slips out of my lips at his touch.

"You'll shave for me tonight," Luca says coldly. "I won't have you staying this unkempt."

I flush at that, my skin burning with humiliation. *I've been in the hospital recovering from being tortured.* I want to snap. *I wasn't thinking about shaving my pussy for you.* But I can't say anything at all because Luca chooses that moment to slide his fingers deeper, and I'm momentarily incapable of speech.

"Little liar," Luca croons, his voice silky as his finger slides up to flick my clit. "You're *dripping* for me, Sofia. So fucking wet." He thrusts two fingers into me, moving them back and forth hard and fast so that I can hear exactly how wet I am, the lewd sounds filling the back of the car. "You can't say you don't want it. I can feel how much you do. I can feel your pussy clenching right now, trying to keep me inside of you."

He says it so casually, reclining back against the leather seat of the car as his fingers thrust in and out of me, as if this is *normal*. As if my husband finger-fucking me in the back of a town car in broad daylight, with only a thin divider between the driver and us, is a perfectly ordinary occurrence.

"You're going to come for me, aren't you, Sofia? If I play with that hard little clit?" His voice is so seductive, sliding up my skin, bathing me in heat, in lust, in *need*. I want to say no, that I'll never come for him again, that he can't make me, that I don't want it, but my traitorous pussy tells a different story. I can *hear* it, smell it, the thick scent of sex filling the back of the car, and I want to beg for more than his fingers. I want to beg for his mouth, his cock, for all of him, for him to make me come over and over the way he has so many times before.

It makes me hate him. I hate that I want him. That I'd let him do every filthy thing he desires even after everything. But all that hate doesn't change how my hips arch up into his hand, how the building pleasure makes me weak, makes me tip my head back, panting as he pushes me closer to a climax.

"That's it, Sofia," he croons, his voice almost mocking. "Come on my fingers. There's a good girl. Come for your husband, show him just how much you want him." He reaches down, adjusting himself, and I can *see* his thick cock in my mind's eye, dripping with arousal, sliding against my entrance, pushing into me, and filling me the way I so desperately crave right now.

He thumbs my clit, rolling it under the pad. "Come for me, sweetheart. Show me how much you crave this."

"I don't—" I gasp, my hips bucking up as he pushes on my clit, his fingers moving faster now, curling inside of me, pressing against that sweet spot. "I don't...fucking...*want you!*"

I shriek the last words, my body spasming as I come hard, unraveling against his hand as the pleasure wracks my body. I can feel myself clenching around his fingers, pulling them deeper, my thighs squeezing around his wrist to hold him there, rubbing my clit as I ride the waves of sensation. It feels so fucking good, my body on fire in an entirely different way. I gasp and moan helplessly as Luca keeps going until I'm pushing at his wrist, trying to shove him away as my clit becomes intensely sensitive in the aftermath.

Luca laughs, yanking his hand out of my panties. He raises his fingers to his nose, breathing in my scent, and for a second, I think he's going to lick them clean. But instead, he shoves them into my face, pressing his fingertips against my lips, smearing my arousal across my mouth as he pushes them inside.

"Not wet for me, hm?" He ignores my muffled whimper, pushing his fingers into my mouth until I have no choice but to wrap my lips around them, tentatively running my tongue over the skin and wincing at my own taste. It's not to my liking, and Luca smirks. "Taste it," he growls. "And then try lying to me again, *wife.*"

He hisses that last word like a curse, leaving his fingers in my mouth until I've licked them clean, and then he pulls his hand free and wipes it on his suit trousers just as the car turns into the parking garage.

"We're home, darling wife," he says, his voice mocking as the car comes to a halt. The moment I'm out, he grabs my elbow, hauling me towards the elevator. He doesn't let go of me until we're in the living room, the scene of so many of our fights, about to be the battlefield for another one.

"Now tell me the truth this time," Luca says, letting go of my arm with a jerk and stepping back, his gaze cold and flinty again. "Why were you at the church, Sofia?"

I can still feel the tingles of the orgasm he just gave me between my legs, but I fight back anyway. *This is just how we are,* I think despondently, even as I raise my chin to glare at him. *We're always going to be like this. Fight and fuck. Fight and fuck.*

Maybe I could live with it, even get some enjoyment from it. I can't honestly say that I don't like the punishments he metes out, that I don't get pleasure from his hands on me, his mouth—

I can't deny that I don't push him to the edge on purpose sometimes. But there's more to think about now than just me.

There's the baby. *Our* baby, *my* baby. And I have to get free of Luca if I'm going to save her.

"I needed to go to confession." I look him straight in the eye as I say it, refusing to back down. "I don't think Father Donahue makes house calls for that."

"He would if I asked." Luca's voice is dangerously soft. "So what did you need to confess, Sofia?"

"That's between him and me." I toss my hair back, wrapping my arms around myself. "I don't have to tell—"

Luca takes a threatening step forwards, closing the space between us again. "See, that's where you're wrong, Sofia. *My* authority over you supersedes everything else. The vow that the priest made. Your privacy. Even God. In this house, *I* am god, Sofia, do you understand me? So tell me, what did you need so badly to confess?"

"I won't—"

"Was it the way you kissed me back that first night up against this door, just for a second before you slapped me?" He points at the front door. "Or was it the way you whimpered and writhed on my fingers when I bent you over this couch?" He gestures to the arm of it, where I remember lying flat on my belly all too well as he teased me to the brink. "Maybe the orgasm you had in front of that poor waiter while I fingered you under the table? Or the way you begged for my cock that night I punished you?" He smiles coldly, and it's almost more frightening than the glare. "Or maybe it's even worse. Maybe you needed to confess how much you secretly liked it the other night when I came home bloody. When I fucked you and covered you in my cum. Is that what you told the priest?"

He reaches out, grabbing my chin in his hand. "Did you tell Father Donahue all your filthy secrets? Everything we do together in bed? Were you so ashamed of it that you had to go running to the priest so he can think about it later while he lies in his cold bed and jerks off to the thought of that pretty face covered in my cum?" Luca yanks his hand away, and I stumble a little, my face going pale.

"No," I whisper. "Nothing like that."

"Oh. Then you must have some secret from me." His eyes lock onto mine, unforgiving and angry. "Is that it? Did you need to confess some secret that you're keeping from your husband?"

"No!"

"I keep hearing that word from your lips today, wife. But I don't think you mean it." He looks down at me. "So you went to church for forgiveness, then? To confess your sins and be absolved, like a good little Catholic girl?"

"Yes." I lick my lips nervously, looking up and hoping that he'll leave it at that. "That's exactly why I went. It's been so long, and after the intruder, I was scared—"

His face hardens at that, and I don't think I've ever seen him look so angry. "So you're scared? You don't think I can keep you safe?"

"I—"

"I can't keep you safe, Sofia, because you won't fucking do as your told." His jaw clenches, the muscle there twitching. "If you wanted to ask forgiveness, you should have been asking it of me, your husband. For not appreciating all I've done, all I've risked, to keep you safe. For stretching the bounds of my patience, over and over again." He reaches down then, undoing the buckle of his belt. "Since you're so concerned with forgiveness, Sofia, let's start there. Get on your knees."

I can see how hard he is, the thick ridge of his cock straining against his fly, wanting to be freed. A part of me, that part that always wants to give in when he's like this, that secretly relishes the punishment, the debasement, intends to do exactly that. I want to sink to his knees, and take him in my mouth, and suck him dry. I want to see him come apart, his cold hard façade cracking when he climaxes, his eyes hot and wild, and hands clutching when he loses control. I want to be the one who makes him do that.

But I can't give in to that part. Not anymore.

"No." This time the word comes out hard and firm, and I mean it. "I'm not doing that, Luca. I'm not playing these games. No more."

To my shock, he starts to laugh. It's a deep, rolling laugh from his gut, and he rubs his hand over his mouth, shoulders shaking as he leaves his belt partially undone, bracing himself against the couch with the other. It sends chills down my spine because I know what's coming next.

More anger.

But when he speaks, his voice isn't angry. Just flat and humorless, without feeling. It's almost worse than the passionate fury of before. "You don't deserve any of this," he says, shaking his head. "You don't deserve to be treated like my wife. I marry you, give you sanctuary, shelter, the best of everything, pleasure beyond anything you would have experienced out there in the world. Do you think any of those shitty Tinder fucks you might have given your virginity to would have made you scream the way I do? Made you beg and plead and come over and over? Fuck no." He grimaces. "You act as if I'm hurting you, as if everything I've done is some terrible burden. You won't listen, won't obey, won't trust my judgment despite the fact that you spent your whole life sheltered from this world and don't know the first thing about surviving it. And now you won't even fucking get me off."

"Luca, I—"

"Shut the fuck up," he snarls, and I can see the tension in every line of his body, see his clenched jaw, his gritted teeth, the thick line of his still-hard cock, and I know he's on the brink of madness.

After everything he did to get you out of there, are you really surprised?

"This isn't fucking worth it," Luca says with a short laugh, shaking his head. "*You* aren't fucking worth it. Maybe Vitto was right after all. I should have just let him fucking kill you."

The words cut deep. They shouldn't, but my hand comes up to cover my mouth before I can stop it, my throat tightening. This is crueler than he's ever been before. This isn't a game.

I think he might actually mean it.

"Or I should have let Viktor have you," he continues. "I'm half inclined to give you to him anyway, see if he still has any fucking use for you. It's a shame, really," Luca says, his eyes trailing up and down my body. "A fucking shame."

I can hardly speak. "What is?"

He laughs again, cold and brittle. "That I took your virginity. At least then, you'd be worth something."

And then, without another word, he turns and stalks away.

Hot tears rise up into my eyes, unbidden and burning at the back of them. This feels worse somehow, than anything he's said to me before. Anything he's done. Because this doesn't feel like him toying with me.

It feels like he really wants to be rid of me. Like he regrets our marriage.

Don't you?

It's an even more loaded question than it ever has been because now this marriage has given me something else. Something that I can cherish and love even if I can't—or won't—love Luca. Even if he won't love me back.

Something I won't let him take away from me.

At least then you'd be worth something. The words beat inside of my skull, tormenting me. What did he mean by that? Did he mean as something to sell, like I'd always thought Viktor intended? It doesn't make sense because I know Luca has always been violently against the Bratva practice of trafficking women. It's one of the things the Italians hold up as a sign of how much more sophisticated they are, that they don't buy and sell people.

They just force them into marriages they don't want.

I know I shouldn't follow him upstairs. I should leave him alone, let him cool down. Let us *both* cool down. But I can't help myself. I want to know what he meant, why he would say something like that, what's driven him to the breaking point. Was it what he saw when he came to save me at the safe house?

Is he angry with me for leaving because, deep down, it's about more than just control?

I go up the stairs two at a time, my heart in my throat as I walk towards the master suite. I don't know what his reaction will be to my following him up here, but I can't just let it go. No matter how much I know, I should.

I almost expected the door to be locked, but it's not. Gingerly, I push it open, peering inside for Luca, but he's not there. Kicking off my shoes, I pad silently across the floor, my toes curling as I tiptoe towards the bathroom, wondering if that's where he's gone. I'm not going to barge in on him or anything, but—

What I see around the corner of the door stops me in my tracks.

Luca is bent over the counter, one hand bracing himself against the mirror as the other strokes his cock furiously, gripping himself tightly as he jerks it hard and fast. The taut flesh gleams in the light, slick with something he's used to lube it first. The sound of his fist meeting skin wetly tightens something deep in my belly, an answering tingle of warmth spreading through my groin and legs.

I've never watched a man do this, never even seen it before outside of the few times I watched porn. I can't stop staring, fascinated by the sight of him, his fist sliding over the thick, throbbing length again and again, over the angry red tip and back down. His movements are harsh, desperate, his feet planted apart. There's nothing sensuous about what he's doing. He's still fully clothed, just his belt undone and zipper pulled down, and something about that makes it even hotter. I can see his reflection in the mirror, his jaw clenched, throat flushed as he strokes himself faster, pushing himself towards his release. I can hear him groaning, panting, his hips thrusting into his fist now as if he's fucking it. I know without a doubt that he's imagining me bent over that counter, that it's my pussy he's driving into with such force, that it's my arousal dripping off of his length, that it's me he's about to come inside of instead of his hand.

With a rush of heady arousal mixed with embarrassment, I realize I'm wet, my panties soaked with it again, and I have the sudden urge to reach up my skirt and touch myself, to bring myself to climax while I watch my husband jerk off without him knowing I'm there. I lean against the wall, telling myself that I'll only brush my inner thigh, only rub my fingers against the outside of my panties, that I just want to find out how wet I really am.

I have to bite my lip hard not to cry out when my fingers slide underneath, rubbing my clit in fast, tight little circles as Luca thrusts into his hand. His expression is almost one of pain instead of pleasure, his green eyes blazing with some dark emotion, and I know that he must be close.

I am too. I'm going to come when he does. I know it. The moment I see him jerk forward, a deep groan spilling from his lips as his cum spills from his cock, I have to shove my fist into my mouth to keep from crying out, grinding against my hand as my legs shake. My knees almost buckle, my own climax washing over me as I watch my husband come into his fist, his hand still jerking erratically until he squeezes every last drop from his pulsing length.

And then, as I watch, Luca looks at his reflection in the mirror, the muscle in his cheek jumping as his jaw clenches hard.

"Fuck!" he screams, his voice filling the room, and his fist slams into the glass. Once, and then twice.

The glass shatters, pieces of it clattering into the sink. His hand flattens against the remnants of the mirror, and I see blood dripping down the glass, trickling over his fingers as he bows his head.

Oh god. Luca. Something in my chest tightens, and I go to him without thinking. The sight of him bleeding and hurt tugs at something deep within me, and I walk into the bathroom, my heart pounding as I approach him cautiously, like you would an injured dog that might bite.

"Luca?" I whisper his name, my voice trembling. "You're hurt. Let me help—"

He whirls to face me, his green eyes bright and glittering with an emotion so dangerous that I stumble backward, suddenly terrified. "Get out!" he roars, clutching his bleeding hand. "Get the *fuck* out!"

I run. I don't know what else to do. I bolt out of the room, down the hall to mine, and slam the door behind me, panting as I lean against it. And then, only then, as I sink to the carpet and bury my face in my hands, do I burst into tears.

LUCA

8

The next day, I call Franco to my office. There's an unexpected guest there as well, already sitting in one of the leather chairs by the time Franco walks in.

Anastasia Ivanova.

"What the fuck is she doing here?" Franco asks, his expression startled. "And what the hell happened to your hand?" He glances at my right hand, which is swathed in gauze and bandages. I didn't bother going to the hospital. A few excruciating minutes with a tweezer getting the pieces of glass out and a first-aid kit later, it ought to heal up alright. It'll probably leave scars, but I don't give a fuck about that.

If I don't figure this out soon, a few scars will be the least of my worries.

"She's here because we have a use for her," I say flatly. "We need to know what Viktor wants. And since he insists on playing coy with me and refusing to give me an answer that I'm willing to entertain, we're going to resort to other methods."

"What, we're going to send *her* in to assassinate him? The fucking ballerina?" Franco snorts. "Good fucking luck."

"Look—" Anastasia starts to say, but I silence her with a glare. She sinks back into the leather seat, her expression mutinous.

"No." I lean back in my chair, looking between the two of them as Franco flops into the seat next to Anastasia. "We've tried intimidation. We've tried pain. We've threatened Viktor and tortured his men, and none of that has worked. So now we try something different." I smile tightly. "Pleasure."

Anastasia's mouth drops open. "What?" Her blue eyes are very round in her pale, delicate face, and it makes me want to laugh. I've looked into her. I did a deep dive into her background when she first became Sofia's roommate when Rossi wanted her killed so that Giovanni's treasured daughter wouldn't be sharing a roof with a 'filthy Russian bitch,' as he so gallantly put it.

The little ballerina immigrated with her mother as a child. After her father was executed for fucking up a mission he was sent on by the *Pakhan* in Moscow. He'd been ordered to clear out an entire family —father, mother, and children—for a crime the father had committed against the Bratva. Anastasia's father was willing to kill the man without question. Perhaps even the wife, after all, she'd helped her husband conceal evidence from the *Pakhan* and known about the money he'd stolen. But the children? He couldn't do that.

He paid for that with his life. Anastasia's mother escaped, taking her daughter to Manhattan, where she'd clearly hoped they could disappear. Of course, there was no disappearing from the Bratva. But they hadn't cared about the dead soldier's bitch and his infant. At first, I'd wondered if Anastasia had been sent to live with Sofia as a means of watching her, reporting back to the Bratva. That had been Rossi's fear. But I hadn't seen any evidence that was the case.

"I saved your life, you know," I say casually. "Rossi wanted you killed when you moved in with Sofia. But I convinced him that you weren't a threat. So I'd say you owe me, little ballerina."

"I have a name." Anastasia glares at me right back. "So what, you want me to fuck Viktor?" She snorts. "That sounds like a good way to die."

"You can die just as easily anywhere else. Accidents happen all the time, every day. You could be walking down the street and *poof—*" I snap the fingers of my good hand. "Something happens. A falling brick. A passerby with a gun. A car that runs a light." I smile coldly at her, making my meaning plain. I can see from her expression that she understands. "But no, not Viktor. I want you to infiltrate the Bratva, yes. I want you to get information from us, from his brigadiers. Seduce them. Convince them to spill secrets while you lie in bed with them and tease them. Men talk when they're distracted with sex."

"You know this for a fact?" Anastasia smirks. "Do you talk, then?"

"That's none of your business." I glare at her.

"Maybe I'll ask Sofia."

"I'd be careful what trouble you get Sofia into these days." I press my lips together thinly. "What do you say? Will you do it?"

"Hold on," Franco interrupts. "You really think this is a solution? Surely they know she's Sofia's friend. What if they put two and two together, and it adds up to us? Viktor won't appreciate—"

"I'm sure he'll appreciate it more than us continuing to return his men in pieces," I say smoothly. "And after all, little Anastasia here isn't known for being chaste. Are you?" I look over at her, the same cold smile still pasted on my face. "You like to sleep around, and visit underground clubs, and jump into bed with questionable men. Isn't that true?"

Anastasia flushes red. "I don't have to sit here and be called a slut by you two assholes," she hisses, pushing herself up out of the chair. "Fuck you."

"Sit down!" My voice thunders in the small room, and even Anastasia, for all her defiance, shrinks back. "You have a choice," I tell her, fixing her with a withering stare. But like Sofia, she doesn't flinch from it. *Neither of these women knows when to back down,* I think grimly. "You can do as I ask, or you can accept the consequences."

"And what are those?" Anastasia looks at me, her expression a challenge, and I realize at that moment the path that I'm headed down.

She can marry you, or she can die. Rossi's voice echoes in my head. *I'm sure you know which one I would prefer.*

I swore that when I became don, I would rule differently. That I would make different choices. And yet, here I am, taking the first steps down the same road.

"You know what fucking happens if you defy us," Franco says, his eyes narrowed, and I whip around to glare at him.

"I didn't ask for input yet." My voice is tight. "When I need backup, I'll let you know."

"Sorry, man." Franco shrugs, but his voice suggests he's not all that sorry.

"What, you're going to kill me?" Anastasia stares at me. "If I don't agree to go fuck some Bratva for you?" She laughs, shaking her head. "Wow, Sofia will *really* fucking hate you after that. You're just *trying* to ruin your marriage, aren't you?"

"I don't think this is a good idea," Franco interjects, and I glare at him, irritated with the second interruption. But I'm surprised, too. It's not as if he gives a shit about Ana. So I can't imagine what his hang-up is with the plan.

"You wanted me to do something about this," I say tightly. "This is me doing something. We'll give Anastasia a small recorder that's easy to hide. It'll pick up anything that her mark says. They shouldn't have any reason to suspect her, especially if she's good at her job—which I wouldn't have suggested this if I didn't think that she would be."

"Thanks. I think," Ana says dryly.

"It's a waste of our time and putting her in unnecessary danger," Franco says, still protesting. "Think of how Sofia will feel if her best friend gets killed because we sent her in to spy on the Russians. You know what they do to spies and traitors. You're really going to put Anastasia in that kind of danger?"

I frown. "I've never known you to be so worried about Sofia or any woman." *You're barely this worried about your wife.*

Franco shrugs, his face, expressionless. "You're the one who said you wanted to be less like Rossi, man."

"Which is why I'm not threatening Anastasia with death," I say wryly.

"You're not?" Her mouth twists, her expression suspicious. "So what if I refuse?"

"Then you refuse. But Anastasia, they're after your best friend. Sofia needs us to protect her." I know what Ana's weakness is. If there's any way to get her to agree to what we want, it'll be by appealing to her love for her friend. She'll be much more likely to agree if she feels that she's doing it for Sofia and not for me.

"You really think this will help her?"

"If we can find out what Viktor might want besides her, or something that we can exploit in exchange for him ceasing the violence against us, then yes. But we've tried to do that by violence. We need to try something different—and you're our best bet for that."

"Because I'm Russian?"

"Yes," I say bluntly. "They'll be willing to believe you're trying to get an inroad into the Bratva, to get protection by becoming the mistress or wife of one of the brigadiers."

Ana licks her lips nervously. "Alright," she says finally. "I'll do it."

"I still think it's too dangerous," Franco starts to say. "There are other ways of accomplishing—"

"Enough!" I shake my head. "I've sheltered you for a long time, Franco. But it's time that you grow up and learn to make the hard choices. We're sending Anastasia into danger, yes. But we send men into danger all the time. She's just as capable." I smile at her, making it as genuine as I possibly can in my current mood. "Right?"

"Sure." Ana frowns. "I swear to god if you get me fucking murdered, Luca—"

"You'll haunt me. Of course." I wave my hand at her.

"I'll reincarnate as fucking Baba Yaga and pull your fingernails out while you sleep," she says, glaring at me. "I know what they'll do to me if they catch me."

"Then don't get caught," I say simply. "If they don't believe that you're trying to attach yourself to a member, then feed them small bits of information. Pretend that you're using your proximity to me through Sofia to betray me. If you need little things that won't be too damaging, let me know, and I'll give you what I can. You're a smart girl, Anastasia. I'm sure you'll be fine."

The look that she gives me tells me that she's not so sure. But at this point, I'm not sure what else to do.

It's time that we all start to take risks.

* * *

THE FIRST MEETING of our families is done at a safe house. Not the same one that I rescued Sofia from—I'm not sure I could walk into that house without wanting to be sick. I've always thought of myself as a tough, hardened man.

But that shook me to my core. Not only because it was my wife, but because of the sheer cruelty, the horror that they'd inflicted on her. I've done terrible things to men, but to an innocent woman?

We all have our lines we won't cross, or so I'd always believed. But that made me wonder if Vitto Rossi had any at all, which unsettles me all the more.

Because he was the man who made me.

I had no doubt that Colin Macgregor would show. The Irish have been close with us for decades, ever since the seventies when a peace was made, and we went into business together instead of fighting one another. There have been a few bumps in the road since then, a few skirmishes and scuffles, but for the most part, the peace has held. I can't imagine that Colin would want to risk that in any way.

But these days, I'm starting to wonder if I truly know anyone around me at all.

The red-haired king of the Irish mob shows at five minutes to the appointed time, however, striding into the room with a confident air that I'm used to when it comes to him. He's the oldest of the three of us, his red hair gone that buttery-white that redheads so often turn in their older age, his jaw covered with a heavy scruff of the same color, sprinkled with a few stubborn red hairs. He's long-nosed and freckled, with keen hazel eyes, and not for the first time, I can't help but notice the resemblances that others have seen between him and Franco.

Those are only coincidences, though. There's a document in the safe in my office proving Franco's paternity, naming his father as Matthias Bianchi. He's Italian blood, through and through. But still—I can see the familiar lines of my best friend's face in Colin's, and it never fails to unsettle me the slightest bit.

I wonder if Viktor will show. If a meeting like this is called, or even more so, an official conclave, then the unspoken law is that all heads of the families must attend, or send a second in their place. It's possible that Viktor will send Levin instead of deigning to come himself, and sure enough, that's what he does. I see the tall, bulky man with white-blond hair and icy eyes walk in, looking dangerously irritated, and do my best not to show my own frustration. I wanted to speak with Viktor, not his second-in-command. But the results will be the same, I imagine. Levin speaks for Viktor, just as Franco could speak for me, or Colin's son Liam could speak for him.

"You know why I've called you here," I say when we're all finally assembled. It's the three of us and security teams for each. I've put Franco in charge of getting Ana the recorder she needs for her job and giving her the instructions I left. It's intentional—I want Franco to understand that I'm not going to be argued with. He can act as my underboss, or there will be consequences. I can't afford to hold his hand any longer.

"The explosion at the hotel, aye?" Colin shrugs. "I didn't have naught to do with it. Nor any of my men. Sounds like Bratva violence to me."

"It wasn't us," Levin says stiffly. "Viktor will not take responsibility. The deaths of the Rossi woman and your other men are on your head. Look to your own people. We will not take the blame."

I can feel the simmering anger that I have had such difficulty holding back lately rising. "I'll give you another chance." My voice is deadly calm. "I want peace. Vitto Rossi may have been bloodthirsty, but I am not. But I will not stand for lies, either."

Colin shrugs. "You know I don't have any desire to break our peace either, brother. But I won't take responsibility for a crime my men and I didn't commit, aye? You can't expect that."

"Are you certain none of your men acted on their own?" I narrow my eyes. "Dissent within the ranks, perhaps? Alliances you're not aware of? Are you sure that all of your men are loyal?"

I see his jaw tighten, his expression flickering dangerously. "I know my men, lad," Colin says, his voice taking on an edge. "You might be don now, Romano, but you're still many years my junior. You want the respect we gave Vitto, you earn it. And questioning my ability to control my men and command loyalty is not the way."

"I didn't mean disrespect," I say calmly, forcing back my anger. "But you understand that I need to bring an end to this. There's been too much blood."

"You're just as bloody as the rest of us," Levin says with a snort. "How much Bratva blood stains the floors of your warehouses? The water runs red with it. You've dumped so many Russian bodies these past months."

"Not nearly as many as we will if this doesn't come to some resolution." I narrow my eyes. "I need answers. So talk, Levin."

He shrugs. "I'm second to the *Pakhan*. I don't take threats, Romano. You won't be pulling pieces off of me. I say we don't have any responsibility for these attacks."

The threads holding my temper together fray and snap as I look at Levin's cool, icy expression, and I feel the hot rage boil through my blood. I have a short fuse these days, shorter than what's advisable, really. But I'm tired of being jerked around. I'm tired of fighting everyone. Rossi had years of peace, and I've inherited this, this—

This absolute shitshow.

"Enough!" I slam my hands down on the table, standing up. "I am the don, and I hold power here! No Irish hold any part of Manhattan or the territory between here and Boston. You hold Boston because we fucking allow it. The Bratva holds what we've graciously let them keep. We could wipe every fucking Russian from the map if I so chose. So here are *my* terms." I look around the room, glaring at every single man assembled. "I need a name by the conclave. If there is no name, there will be war among our three families. I will stop at nothing to destroy everyone who might have been involved. I say that now, here, as we're assembled formally. A name or there will be blood."

Colin shifts in his seat. "You said you didn't want war, lad. But your words now say otherwise."

"I don't *want* war," I repeat. "But the time has come, clearly, for me to assert my place among you, and yes—my place above you. So I say it now, again."

My eyes flick to Levin, and then back to Colin. And when I speak, I mean it down to my bones.

"The name of the one responsible. Or I kill you all."

SOFIA

9

I need Ana.

It took some effort on my part, but I figured out how to get the iPad's password broken so that I could connect it and send a text. I know I'll see Caterina this week, but she's weighed down by everything that's happened to her family. Besides, I know that there's only one person who I can really trust with my secret.

My best friend.

When Ana walks in, she takes one look at me and walks straight to me, pulling me into an embrace as she rubs her hand over my back, squeezing me tightly. "Does Luca know I'm here?" she murmurs quietly as she hugs me, and I shake my head.

"No. I figured out how to text you on my own."

"Let's go talk in the bathroom, then," Ana says into my ear. "There are no cameras in there, right?"

"God, I fucking hope not."

That's how we find ourselves in the huge bathroom off of my room, sitting on the warm tile with our backs against the jacuzzi tub. It seems oddly poignant since I've thrown up so many times in here since figuring out that I must be pregnant. I lean my head back, looking sideways at my best friend.

"Something's wrong, isn't it?"

"Yeah." I laugh. "Something is really fucking wrong."

"Is it Luca?" Ana reaches over and slides her fingers between mine. "Is he hurting you?"

"Not—exactly. I mean, he's not easy to live with, that's for sure. But he's not like…hitting me or anything, if that's what you mean." I can't begin to tell her about the mind games he plays with me in bed because then I'd have to explain that sometimes I like it, that I'm both repulsed and turned on by the way we fight with each other, and that nothing in my life has ever confused me as much as Luca does.

"Then what?" Ana asks, looking at me with real worry written across every inch of her face, and it makes me want to crumble. I've felt alone for what feels like so long now and seeing my friend ready to listen, to help me if she can, sitting here in the small warm sanctuary of my bathroom, I feel as if I can tell someone my secret.

I can at least tell her.

"I'm pregnant." The words come out in a whisper, hanging in the space between us, and Ana's jaw literally drops as she stares at me.

"Oh god, Sofia." Ana claps her hand to her mouth. "What are you going to do? Does Luca know?"

"No! And you can't say anything. He—" I pause, feeling sick all over again.

"I would never," Ana promises. "You know that. But why do you look terrified? Surely Luca would be happy…that's a possible heir for him. Isn't that what all these macho mob men want? Sons to prove that they're virile and can pass all this shit on?" She waves her hand around to indicate the penthouse and Luca's wealth.

I shake my head, chewing on my lower lip. "The contract he made me sign—there was a clause in it saying that I can't get pregnant. If I do, then I'm supposed to terminate the pregnancy immediately or lose everything. Luca's protection, my rights as his wife, everything. If I don't—then the contract between us is void. The agreement to keep me alive is void."

Ana's expression is more horrified than I've ever seen it. "Oh, Sofia," she whispers. "Why?"

"I don't know," I say miserably, shaking my head. "I don't understand it."

"Why did you agree to it?"

"I didn't really have much of a choice. But I also didn't plan to sleep with him, remember? I made him agree to leave me a virgin. But then Rossi interfered and made sure that we'd have to. And after that—"

"You guys did it again?" Ana's eyes go even rounder. "Sofia, normally I'd congratulate you on finally getting laid and enjoying it, but this—what changed? You were so sure—"

"I don't know," I admit. "There was the intruder, and Luca came flying straight home from Franco's bachelor party when he heard. I was so traumatized and afraid, and Luca just came riding in like some kind of white knight. I know—I *knew*—he's anything but that. But I forgot for just a minute. A lot of minutes, actually," I admit, my face flushing red. "A *lot* of them."

"And that was the only time?"

"No," I say, my face burning even hotter. "But it's the night we didn't use a condom. And there was one other time we didn't, but—I know it was that night. I just wasn't thinking—"

"God, Sofia." Ana shakes her head. "What are you going to do?"

"I don't know." I bite my lip again, trying not to cry. "I need a way out. I tried to go to Father Donahue, and he was going to help me—but then I was kidnapped from the church. And now Luca has an even tighter hold on me, more security—I'm not going to get away again. But if I start to show—" Tears do well up in my eyes then, before I can stop them. "I have to do something, Ana. I have to save my baby."

Ana just watches me, her eyes wide and sad, and I can see from the expression on her face that she's every bit as much at a loss as I am. "I don't know what to tell you, Sofia. Luca's going to find out that I came to visit you, and maybe he'll be angry and maybe he won't. It's impossible to tell with him. But I saw the security he's got around this place and inside of it, and I don't know how you could possibly leave again. He's got you good and caged." She bites her lip. "I'm sorry. I don't even know what to think of him anymore. I thought he was doing it to protect you, but now—I can't believe he made you promise that."

"I have an idea," I whisper. "I came up with it this morning. But I'd need your help. And I don't want to ask you to put yourself in danger for me—"

Ana snorts. "Sofia, Luca's already asked me to do exactly that."

"What?" I stare at her in confusion. "What do you mean?"

"Luca asked me to infiltrate the Bratva," Ana says flatly. "He wants me to sleep with some of the brigadiers and see if I can get anything out of them. A regular Mata Hari." She shrugs. "He said it was to help you. To find out what Viktor wants so that he can figure out how to make peace. Before something worse happens."

"Something worse is *going* to happen if I don't find a way out."

"I think Luca does care about you." Ana hesitates. "But—"

"It doesn't matter what he feels for me anymore," I insist. "All that matters is protecting my baby. He's moody. You've seen that. He's more married to the mafia than he ever will be to me. Do you think he'll choose our baby and me over what he's been working for all his life? I don't even know *why* he insisted on that clause, but there must be a reason."

"So, what can I do?" Ana looks at me, her mouth twisting with worry. "I'm already going into danger. So if I can help, Sofia, I will. You know I'd do anything for you. And my loyalty will always be to you over anyone else."

"I know." I squeeze her hand. "You're my best friend. When I put out that ad for a roommate, I never thought that I'd find someone that I'd be so close to. You're more than that—you're the sister I never had."

"I feel the same way." Ana tilts her head sideways, laying it on my shoulder for a moment before sitting up and looking at me, her eyes serious. "So tell me what you need."

I take a deep breath and explain the idea I came up with this morning. It's not great, but it's all I have.

"I don't want Luca dead," I say quietly. "He's the father of my child, and I—my feelings about him are complicated. I know that I don't want him to die, though. But if the Bratva could help me without that—my mother was Russian. I have Russian blood in my veins, and maybe if Viktor knew that, he might help me for her sake."

"Do you think Viktor doesn't already know?"

I shrug. "Does the Bratva sell Russian girls?"

"I don't know." Ana chews on her lower lip. "So if he doesn't know, you think that it might help you?"

"It might. I don't know. But maybe he would. They wanted me in the first place to get to Luca. So maybe I can give them something without actually getting him killed. It's all I can think of," I say helplessly. "I don't know what else to do. I'd never ask you this otherwise—I'd try to get Luca to not have you do what he's asking. But I'm desperate." The last words come out as a whisper; they're hard to even say aloud. I've tried so hard to be strong through all of this, but I can feel myself breaking.

"I'll try to find out anything that I can," Ana promises, squeezing my hand. "I'll see if I can get any information about what they wanted with you beyond getting to Luca. And if I can do anything to get you out of here, I will."

"Thank you," I whisper. "This means so much to me, Ana, I—"

"Listen," she says urgently. "This is dangerous, Sofia. *Really* dangerous. You don't want to imagine what the Bratva will do to me if they figure this out. I have to play this perfectly, or I'm dead. *Worse than dead.* Do you understand?"

I nod, my throat tight. I haven't told Ana what happened to me in the safe house, but I understand better than she knows. "What do you need from me?"

"I need you to make Luca believe you're sorry. That you're not going anywhere. That you're going to obey him, and do as he asks, and be the perfect little mafia wife, until I can figure something out for you. Seduce him, make him happy, anything you have to do. Just don't fight with him or antagonize him. Well," she amends, "maybe a little bit. If you become totally submissive, he'll *really* know something is up." Ana laughs, but there's not much humor in it. "Just—make him think that you've learned your lesson. Can you do that?"

Before now, I would have said no. Everything in me would have rebelled at being an obedient little wife. But now, things are different. And if Ana is going to go into the Bratva, fuck their brigadiers to get information, put herself in that kind of danger—the least I can do is charm and have sex with my husband, who is both gorgeous and turns me on, even if I hate it sometimes.

"Yes," I say quietly. "I can do that."

"Good." Ana smiles at me. "I'm going to help you, Sofia. I promise. We're in this together, okay? I'll do everything I can to make sure you and your baby get out of here safely." She looks down at my stomach. "It's weird thinking that you're pregnant. Jesus, you're not even twenty-two."

"I know." I lick my lips nervously. "I don't know how to be a mother. I'm afraid I'm going to be a terrible one. Especially if I'm on my own—"

"That's the first step in being a good parent, I think," Ana says. "If you're worried about being one. It's going to be okay. Just one day at a time." She takes a deep breath. "I know that's the only way I'm getting through this."

* * *

I DON'T WASTE any time. When Luca comes home, I stay out of his way until I hear him go into the master suite and the sound of the shower turning on. The moment I hear that, I walk into the bedroom, stripping out of the designer joggers and tank top that I'd had on all day, tossing them onto the floor with my heart pounding in my chest. I've given in to Luca plenty of times, even welcomed his advances during that brief period of time where things actually seemed like they were working between us. But I haven't initiated. I haven't tried to seduce him. I wonder if even my doing that will set off alarms for him, and I know I have to be careful about how I do it. I need to be convincing—this has to be the best acting of my life. Never mind that I haven't exactly done much of that.

The memory of what happened this morning flashes through my

head. *I might not have to act that much after all.* Regardless of everything else, it's clear that I'm still attracted to him and as conflicted as ever.

Luca's back is to the shower door, his hands in his hair as he runs soap through the thick dark locks. I take a deep breath as I pad naked towards the shower, opening the glass door and stepping inside.

"Luca," I say quietly.

He whirls around from under one of the two showerheads, soapy water dripping into his eyes. He runs his hand over his face, dashing it away as he stares at me, a truly shocked expression on his face. "Sofia." His voice is cold, without a trace of gentleness. "What the fuck do you think you're doing?"

Okay, so he's closed off to me. It's nothing I haven't seen before. Trying to slow my racing pulse, I take another step towards him, putting my hands on his chest. I can feel his heartbeat, hard and steady behind the wall of muscle, feel him flex beneath my hands as he stiffens.

"What are you doing?" he repeats, looking down at me with suspicion in those green eyes. *He really is gorgeous,* I think, taking in the chiseled cheekbones, the strong jaw, the muscled arms, water dripping down all of it, down his chest and into the lines at his hips, deep cuts of muscle that lead down to—

He's hard and thick already, just from seeing me naked. It gives me a sense of power, a feeling that I'm not completely helpless in all of this. I run my hands down his chest, down to his abs, looking up into his eyes with what I hope is a contrite expression.

"You were right earlier," I say softly. I let my voice tremble a little; he'll expect that of me. I've never been a practiced seductress. He'll expect nerves, hesitation. I don't have to pretend that I'm not afraid, and that's a relief, at least. "I should be asking you for forgiveness."

"Oh?" The question hangs between us, and I can see the suspicion still written across his face. "For what?"

"For running away." I lick my lips, and I see his gaze flick down to them, hanging there for a moment before sweeping down the rest of my body and back up. "For making you worry. For making you have to come and save me, to do everything you did—"

He catches my roving hands in his, squeezing them almost to the point of pain. "Why don't I believe you, Sofia? You'll have to try harder than that to convince me."

"I know I was wrong," I whisper. "I panicked. You came home bloody, and then the rough sex, the way you treated me—it scared me, Luca. I thought we were—"

"In love?" His voice is mocking. "I knew you were stupid, but I didn't think you were that childish."

"No, I—I'm sorry," I whisper it again, looking up at him pleadingly. I don't have to act after all, because I am begging him. Begging him to believe me, to give in, to let me seduce him and make him believe that I want to be here. "Let me make it up to you."

"And how are you going to do that?" Luca raises an eyebrow, arching it as he looks down at me without a trace of emotion. Without hesitation, I sink down to my knees, feeling the warm floor beneath them as I reach up, bracing myself on his hip with one hand as I reach for him with the other. His cock throbs against the palm the moment I wrap my fingers around his length, hard and hot and ready, and I can't pretend that it doesn't feel good to know that I turn him on. That he wants me. *Me.* This man, who has had any woman he's ever wanted, thinks I'm beautiful. Sexy. *Desirable.*

He said I was like a drug to him, more than once. That he felt obsessed with me, addicted to me. That he couldn't stop wanting me.

I'm starting to think that the addiction runs both ways.

Because I feel it too.

I should hate him, but as I lean forward and brush my lips over him, I can feel the hot arousal burning in the pit of my stomach, spreading out through my veins, seeping into my blood. He tastes good, the salty slickness of his pre-cum spreading over my lips, and it makes me feel dirty and sexy and sensual all at once as I run my tongue over and around him, hearing him groan. *I'm not powerless,* I think to myself as I take an inch into my mouth and then another, rolling my eyes upwards to look at his slackened face and glazed expression, pleasure written over every inch of his face. His hand goes into my hair as I push forward, grabbing onto his hips with both hands as I take more and more of his thick cock, determined to get it all into my mouth and down my throat, to feel him lose control.

Both of his hands tangle in my hair as I push him deeper, choking a little as I feel his fingers press into my scalp, his moans filling the humid space of the shower as I hold myself at the base for just a moment, my nose brushing his abdomen before I slide back up, watching him as I run my tongue over his shaft the whole way, teasing him beneath the sensitive head as I gasp for breath.

"That's right," Luca groans. "Suck me off on your knees, wife. Show me just how sorry you are." My hand slides between his legs, cupping his balls as I run my thumb over the fragile skin, gently hefting them in my palm as I sink down again, my lips tightening around him as I feel him throb in my mouth.

I keep going, teasing and licking and sucking. I lose myself in it, in the soapy musky scent of his skin and the feeling of him in my hands and mouth, his taut, hot skin burning against my tongue, the slick taste of him gathering there as I go faster, my hands running up his thighs and over his hips as I give in to the urge to feel him, to learn him even more, to take some pleasure in this. I know I'm wet, my folds are swollen and slick with my own arousal as I go down on him. It's impossible not to be aroused as I look up at the chiseled god of a man looming over me, every inch of his body straining with desire, his moans pushing my desire to an even greater height. He feels good, and I want him. I want more. I know at that moment how easily I could lose myself in my own game, how easily I could start to fall for him again, and I know that I'm going to have to be careful.

"Fuck, Sofia—" Luca groans out my name as his hand tightens in my hair, pushing my mouth down as his hips thrust forward. He doesn't bother warning me, but I know from his reactions that he's about to come, from the way the muscles in his thighs go rigid under my hands. His body pitches forward, his other hand bracing himself against the wall as his hips jerk erratically, the first hot spurt of his cum filling my mouth. I swallow convulsively, taking all of it as he keeps thrusting, still sucking until he pulls away, still shuddering with pleasure as some of the focus comes back into his eyes.

I stand up unsteadily, but before I can say or do anything, Luca grabs me, pushing me back against the tiled wall as his hand tangles in my hair again, his mouth crashing down on mine.

It's not a gentle kiss, not a loving one. His tongue forces its way into my mouth, shoving, claiming, and I can feel his half-hard cock against my thigh as his hand makes its way between my legs. "Wet," he says triumphantly when his fingers plunge inside of me, not even bothering to take a moment to ease me into it, but it doesn't matter. I'm flushed and swollen and aroused, already aching for him, and I cry out against his mouth as his fingers work in and out of me, his thumb pressing against my clit as he grinds himself against my thigh. I can feel the anger in his forceful kiss, his nose bumping against mine, teeth clashing as he grabs my waist suddenly and spins me around, forcing me up against the wall as his fingers dive between my legs again.

"I'm going to make you come," he growls into my ear, and it almost sounds like a threat. His mouth presses against my neck, biting, sucking all the way down, down into the crook of my shoulder as his fingers plunge in and out of my soaking wet pussy. I can feel myself clenching around him, pulling him in, wanting more. My legs spread open, my back arching, ass pressing into his groin, and I know there's no point in fighting it. My body has taken over, and my body wants Luca.

"Please," I whisper helplessly. "Please—"

"Please, what?" He sucks on my neck again, hard, driving his fingers into me. "Please let you come? Please fuck you? Please give you my cock? What do you want?" His fingers slow as he brings me to the edge of orgasm, his thumb sliding off of my clit, and I mewl in protest, rubbing against him.

"You have to tell me," he says, and I can hear the mocking tone in his voice. He likes making me beg for it, likes making me need him. Likes hearing how much he turns me on.

"Please let me come," I whisper, although I could have said any of those things, and it would have been true. "Please—"

"Well, since you asked so nicely."

His thumb presses against my clit again, rubbing, stroking, and that combined with his fingers, with the hard press of his body against my back, the feeling of his hardening cock against my ass, drives me wild. I can feel the orgasm growing, tightening my muscles. Then it explodes without warning, washing over me in waves of pleasure that make me feel as if my knees will buckle. I can't hold myself up, and I feel Luca's arm go around my waist, tightening as I buck and writhe against him, moaning helplessly. The pleasure feels all-consuming, almost too good, and when I feel him spreading my legs wider, bending me over as he moves between my thighs, there's no thought of trying to stop him. It's not even about seducing him anymore, tricking him—I just want it.

It's all real at that moment. The moan when I feel him slide into me, hard and hot and thick, the way my back arches, my nails scratching at the tile as I grind back against him, wanting more, wanting all of it. I want the hard thrust of him into me, again and again, filling me, the way he bites at my shoulder, the groans that spill from his mouth. "Fuck, you're tight," he murmurs, his breath warm against my ear as he pounds into me from behind. "Like a fucking virgin every time." He sucks my lobe into his mouth, his hands running over my waist, my hips. "I love that it's only my cock that's been in you. The only one you know. And you feel so fucking good—"

"So do you," I moan, and I mean it. This is the catch, the thing that fucks me up every time because he *does* feel good. He feels right. In these moments, I don't want to leave. I want to stay, and if we could stay in this moment forever, wrapped in the sultry heat of the shower with the water streaming down over us, his body molded to mine as he plunges into me again and again, I would. If there was no future, only now, repeating over and over again.

But this will end. I can feel it on the verge of ending, his thrusts becoming more erratic, my body tightening, and I cry out. "Let me come one more time," I beg. "Make me come, Luca, please—"

He thrusts again, all the way, rolling his hips against me, and the sound I make is almost a scream as the second orgasm crashes over me. Luca pushes me forward, up against the wall as he holds my shuddering body there, grinding against me as I come hard on his cock, squeezing every inch of him. I don't want him to pull out; I want him to stay inside of me, to come inside of me, but he doesn't have a condom, and he doesn't know that I'm already pregnant.

I whimper when he pulls out, and Luca groans, breathless as I hear the sound of his hand fisting his cock. "On your knees," he growls. "I want to come in your mouth again while you taste yourself on me."

I don't even think about it as I fall to my knees again. I'm lost in a haze of pleasure, my body still faintly pulsing with it, and I take him in my mouth, tasting myself on him as my tongue runs over his length. In my arousal, it almost tastes good. It turns me on, knowing that he's been inside of me, that it's me that's pushed him to the brink, me that's making him come now, as he grabs a fistful of hair and groans with an almost painful sound, his cum spilling out across my tongue and down my throat for the second time tonight.

When he's finally finished, I stand up weakly, my heart still racing. Luca eyes me, and I can still see caution in his face, but the sex has taken the edge off for him. I can tell that much. "If that's how you apologize," he says hoarsely, "maybe I should let you get in trouble more often."

I blink at him, covering my mouth with my hand to stifle a laugh, but then *he* smirks, and I realize he's intentionally making a joke. It happens so rarely—we fight and fuck, but if there's one thing that was missing even from that brief span of time where things felt okay, it was laughter.

I've rarely laughed with Luca. And as we both start to—tentatively, not fully—I feel as if I'm being given another tiny glimpse into how things could be if they were different.

But of course, they're not. And I have to remember what I'm doing here.

"I want to stay tonight," I say softly, slipping back into my role as I lean against him, running my hands over his chest. "In bed with you. I want to come back to our bed."

Luca smooths his hand over my wet hair, and I can feel him relenting, letting his guard down. *Good.* "Alright," he says. "It'll be good not to sleep alone."

That admission is surprising, coming from him. But I don't let him see the surprise on my face.

Later, as I lie on my side of the bed with the lights off, Luca already asleep far away on the other side, I turn my head and look at all the space between us. There was a time when I thought I could bridge that gap. I look at Luca's face, softer in sleep, and try to imagine us as different people.

I try to imagine him with a baby, something that I've never done before. It's almost impossible to do. I try to picture him holding an infant, spoon-feeding a toddler, helping our son or daughter with their homework. None of it fits with the image of the Luca I know. There's not enough love in him for me—or at least so he says, so what would there be for a child?

I think of Caterina, raised all her life to know that anything she tried to do for herself—a degree, an education, a career—would be rendered meaningless by the life that had been chosen for her. If I stayed with Luca, somehow, and we had this baby, what future would he or she have? A son would be raised to take over, to steep himself in the same blood and death that Luca has. I think of my adult son coming home bloody the way Luca did, of him torturing men, making them beg and cry before he killed them. My stomach turns over with nausea that has nothing to do with pregnancy.

But would a daughter be any better? I think of my daughter raised to know that her life hinges on a man, on a marriage, that she'll be given away to whoever is the most advantageous match as if we were living hundreds of years ago and not in modern New York City.

I can imagine exactly what kind of life our children would have here. It's a life that my father tried to get me out of, only for me to be trapped in it.

I can't let my child suffer the same fate, I think, touching my belly in the darkness, with no one here to see. *I have to be stronger.*

Not for the first time, I wonder why he didn't leave. It must have had something to do with loyalty, with friendship, his ties to Rossi and the mafia, and his friend Marco at odds with his loyalty to his family. I can feel that same choice straining at me, because like it or not, I have feelings for Luca that aren't just hate. And it won't be easy to not only leave, but betray him.

It was one thing to run to Father Donahue. It's another altogether to run to Viktor and the Bratva.

I roll onto my side, squeezing my eyes shut. I need rest. I need to sleep.

But with so many unknowns looming ahead of me, I know it's going to be a long night.

LUCA

10

With the date for the conclave set, there's a tentative cease-fire among our families. I never entirely trust Viktor to follow the unspoken etiquette of the mob families, but when peace talks are imminent, the violence is supposed to temporarily be on hold. I don't let my guard down entirely, but it does allow me to shift my focus to other things momentarily, like preparing Ana to go after her first mark in the Bratva.

I gave her the names of the men I wanted her to seek out, as well as the clubs and bars they frequent, and anything else I could dig up on them—the kind of women they usually are seen with, what those women wear, etcetera. Ana showed me her outfit for the first night for approval as requested—a tight black dress that barely covered her to the tops of her thighs with fishnet cutouts at the waist and a plunging neckline.

"Do you want to see the panties too, or will this do?" she'd asked sarcastically, which I'd pointedly ignored. She'd made it clear that she wasn't going to be a submissive employee of mine, and I'm fine with that. As long as she does her job. And since it's for Sofia, I feel confident that she will.

Sofia is with Caterina in the movie room, watching some stupid rom-com, and I pace our bedroom, the one place I know I won't run into them together. I can't easily face Caterina these days, knowing that it was my hand that pulled the trigger that killed her father, and I'm in no mood for small talk.

Ana is supposed to get in touch with me when she leaves afterward, which I imagine will be fairly late. If I haven't heard from her by the time Sofia goes to bed, I'll wait in my office, but for now, I pace the room, trying not to think of all the ways that this could go wrong.

It's not just that Anastasia's life is in danger. It's that if she's discovered, and *my* part in sending her is discovered, this will backfire explosively. Not only will there no longer be any chance of peace, but Viktor will also have all the justification he needs to come after us guns blazing. It'll be a war the likes of which Manhattan hasn't seen in decades.

But if she succeeds—then I might have something I can use. Something that will enable me to put an end to this. And to me, the risk is worth it.

As I pace, I can't help but think of what she's doing. I've never been particularly attracted to Anastasia in that way—she's too thin for my taste, small-breasted to the point of being entirely flat-chested and with an attitude to rival Sofia's—but as I run over the plan, again and again, I picture her on the dance floor of some underground club, grinding on a Bratva man, tossing her hair back and pretending to be infatuated with him. I picture her in bed, that long, thin, pale body stretched out under one of the Russians, and in my mind, she shifts to Sofia.

It's Sofia I see, trapped under one of them, fighting to get away. The image blurs with the one of her bound in the safe house, a picture I can never unsee, and I grit my teeth, trying to force myself to think of anything else. I can feel that old possessive urge rising, the addiction to her, the need to know that she's *mine*. That no one else can touch her, not ever again.

Mine, mine, mine.

I think of her last night, soft and apologetic, looking up at me with those wide dark eyes, the way my body reacted to her, and just like that, I'm hard again. And not just casual arousal, but raging, aching, a feeling that sweeps over me and makes me feel as if I'm hovering on the edge of madness all over again.

At that moment, I understand something. The times that I've hated Sofia, that I've felt pushed to the brink of rage by her, have been the times that she's tried to leave, tried to break her promises, lied to me. The times when *she's* been the one taking away what's mine.

Her.

But other times—I've felt something very different for her. Something that I'm afraid to put a name to because it's so different than anything else I've felt before.

What I felt when I'd heard about the break-in, and I'd come rushing back to her. What I'd felt when I arranged for that night on the rooftop.

Memory after memory floods in as I sit there on the edge of the bed, of Sofia's pale face when I'd flown home, of the shock and joy in her expression on the rooftop, the moments we'd shared together in the theater room, or eating a meal together. For a brief time, I'd had a window into what it's like to really have a relationship with someone, to wake up with them and come home to them, and go to bed with them—and it was better than I'd thought it would be.

It was *good*.

She was good. We were good.

I think of us in the shower last night, laughing, Sofia's hand clapped over her mouth, and my chest tightens. I don't know how to reconcile that with the memory of her on that bed in the safe house, knowing that my loving her, that my letting her into my life fully could easily result in that happening again. I don't know how to have both—her safe and protected as I promised I would, and her as my wife, truly.

But god, I want her more than I want to breathe. And if I'm honest with myself, if I look deeply into the part of myself that I try to keep shuttered away—I love her.

It's not just her beauty, or how much she turns me on. She makes me feel all those things—desire, arousal, lust—more than any other woman I've ever been with, that's true. But it's more than that. It's the way she challenges me, the way she refuses to back down. It's the way she survived something so terrible that it should have broken almost anyone, but not only did she live through it, it didn't break her spirit either. She didn't come back to me as a shell of a person.

She's still Sofia. Still the woman I married, if not more so. There's a strength in her that, if she were free to be herself, to take her place at my side and rule the family with me, could be formidable.

Together, we could be powerful.

But in order for that to happen, she has to be safe.

My hands tighten on the side of the bed, my heart pounding and the need for her still pulsing through me. I have to *make* her safe. I have to win this, no matter what it takes, so that I have a chance at something that I never thought I'd want.

A real marriage with my wife.

The frustration turns to a need for sex, like it always seems to. Since I was a teenager, that's been my escape. My means of forgetting about the things I had to do for Rossi, the things I still have to do for the family that I've belonged to since I was born. My way of escaping my demons for a little while so that I didn't have to think. Didn't have to feel anything but pleasure.

Until Sofia.

I want her *now*. I want to bury myself in her, to slake the addictive need for her scent, her body, the sounds she makes when I drive into her again and again. But she's with Caterina right now, and although I suppose I *could* go in there and drag Sofia out, I'm sure Caterina would be horrified.

Sofia probably wouldn't be all that pleased, either.

I reach down, rubbing the hard ridge of my erection, desperate for some relief. My own hand isn't what I want. I'm on the verge of just trying to distract myself with something else until I look down and see some of Sofia's discarded clothes on the floor at the foot of the bed.

Normally I'd be irritated with her for leaving her things strewn around like that—I have a housekeeper, but I try to keep things tidy in the meantime. I can't stand clutter or mess. But it's not the fact that she left her clothes on the floor that grabs my attention.

It's the pair of silky panties atop her jeans that I can't look away from.

Even as I reach for them, I know that this is insane. I'm reminded of just before we were married, when I stood in her closet with her dress pressed to my nose as I stroked myself to a frustrated climax, except now it feels even worse because I'm not wondering any longer what it would be like to be with her.

I've *had* her, and it was better than I'd ever imagined. So good that I can't just toss her aside like every other woman I've ever had. Instead, I want more. Every day. Every moment that I'm away from her.

Every second of the day, I'm like a frustrated teenage boy, and there doesn't seem to be any cure for it.

Before I know it, I have my belt undone and my cock out, throbbing in my fist as I breathe in Sofia's scent, thinking of her pressed against my face, the sweet taste of her under my tongue, the way she whimpers and writhes when I lick her. Nothing gets me harder than the taste of pussy, and Sofia's is like a drug, better than any Viagra could ever be. Just the thought has me rock-hard and aching. I groan as I stroke myself, slowly first and then harder, faster, as I imagine Sofia underneath me, her thighs wrapped around my head, her hands in my hair as she loses control, all of that good-girl façade washed away as she gives in to her desires and lets me know just how badly she wants it.

The familiar buzz of pleasure takes over, blurring my senses, letting me sink into the fog of it as I wrap the silky panties around my shaft, my balls tightening with the familiar thrill of approaching climax. *That's it,* I think, closing my eyes and imagining that the silky, slippery sensation around my cock is Sofia's warm mouth, or better yet—

"Luca?" Sofia's voice jolts me out of the fantasy, and my eyes fly open, my hand freezing on my shaft. Her eyes flick from my face to my cock, with her panties wrapped around it, soaked with my pre-cum, and I expect her to look horrified, or maybe cry, or run away.

What I absolutely don't expect is what happens next.

"You should have come and found me if you were that horny," she says in a teasing voice, pushing the door shut behind her and walking towards me. In my heightened state of arousal, everything about her looks even better than usual—her curvy hips in those tight jeans, her narrow waist, the swell of her breasts against the black t-shirt she's wearing. Her hair is up in a high ponytail, bouncing against her shoulders as she walks, and I want to grab onto it, hold it as I bend her over, and drive into her from behind.

Fuck. Her eyes are on my cock, and although I never thought I was one for exhibitionism, it's turning me on even more.

"I couldn't interrupt you," I say hoarsely. "You were with Caterina."

"She went home." Sofia's voice lowers a little, dropping into a more sultry register. "I didn't know you were up here."

I can't even form words. My brain doesn't seem connected to my mouth any longer, my cock still throbbing angrily in my fist, and all I want to do is finish. My balls ache, my brain is fogged, and I'm so horny I can't think straight. But I don't know what to do with Sofia standing there.

Having my wife walk in on me while I'm jerking off is a whole new experience for me.

But then, to my amazement, she reaches down and strips her shirt off, tossing it to meet the formerly discarded clothes on the floor.

When her bra joins it, I feel like I might come on the spot.

Sofia has the most perfect breasts. Full but not too big, with perfect dusky pink nipples that are already hardening in the faint chill of the room. They bounce a little as she tosses her bra aside, and at that moment, I'd give anything to have my mouth on them.

"You can keep jerking off with my panties if you want," she says, her hands going to the button of her jeans. "Or you can let me help. Your choice."

Fuck. My brain almost short-circuits with desire. I don't think I've ever heard a hotter sentence in my life. Suddenly, I'm not sure why I ever didn't want to be married, if it's going to be like this.

There's a tiny warning alarm in the back of my head that says this isn't Sofia's usual way of behaving—not seducing me in the shower last night and begging my forgiveness quite literally on her knees or this sexy show that she's giving me now as she wiggles her jeans down her hips, her eyes fixed lustfully on my rock-hard length. *She wants something,* that small, suspicious voice in my head says. *She's playing a game.*

But even if that's true, right now, I don't care. I just need to come. I'm on the verge of blue balls, my cock throbbing and leaking pre-cum so heavily that Sofia's panties, wrapped around the tip, are as soaked as if I already came in them. She could have any reason in the world for wanting to sit on my cock right now, and I wouldn't tell her no. She could drain every bank account I have, so long as she drained my balls at the same time.

This is how men lose everything, I think grimly, but I'm beyond caring as Sofia approaches me, completely naked now, her full breasts bouncing and hips swaying, and I can see the faint arousal between her legs, her lips puffy and pink as she reaches out and pushes me back onto the mattress.

"You're overdressed," she says softly, reaching for my pants and pulling them down my hips. I let go of my cock as she does, looking up at her gorgeous face, her dark hair tumbling around it as her eyes twinkle mischievously down at me, and those ruined panties join the growing pile of clothes on the floor as well as she straddles me, reaching for the buttons of my shirt.

"I need you," I growl, grabbing her hips. My cock is just at her entrance, her pussy hovering above me, and I can feel the heat of her skin. I feel as if I'm going mad, and I can't wait for her to get my shirt off. I need her *now*.

"Oh!" Sofia moans as I pull her downwards, my hips thrusting up at the same time so that my cock impales her, sliding into her tight channel as I feel her clench around me. Her hands flatten on my chest, bracing herself, and she grins down at me as she throws her hair over one shoulder.

"So impatient." She leans down, her hips already starting to rock against me as her mouth brushes over mine. "Alright, fine. Have it your way."

Her riding me is like heaven. I lose myself in the pleasure of it, of her hips in my hands, her hot pussy enveloping me, her palms against my bare chest, nails scratching as she kisses me hard, her tongue tangling with mine. It feels so good, but I need more. I need to be in control, the one claiming her, possessing her, reminding her who she belongs to.

I grab her waist and roll her onto her back, pushing her back against the pillows as I hook her legs over my shoulders. "Watch me," I rasp, spreading her thighs open as I pull out slowly. It takes effort to not just fuck her hard and fast, spilling into her in a matter of seconds, but I want to make it last. It feels so fucking good, and I don't want it to end. "Touch yourself." I reach for her hand, pressing it between her legs. "I want you to make yourself come on my cock."

Sofia is flushed, aroused, beautiful, her eyes flicking down obediently to watch me sliding in and out of her, my thick cock filling her to her limit, her lips spread around me like a blossoming flower. She moans, her soft mouth parted as she watches me, her fingers rubbing her clit in those tiny, tight circles that I know she loves so much, pushing herself to the edge along with me.

"This feels so good," she gasps. "Come with me, Luca, please, I'm so close—"

I should stop, put a condom on, but I can't. I can't make myself pull out of the tight, hot squeeze of her body, like velvet running up and down the length of me, and I'm past caring. *If I knock her up, we'll figure it out,* I think dizzily because, at that moment, there's nothing up to and including a gun to my head that could make me stop fucking her until I finally climax.

"Yes, oh god, Luca, I'm going to—"

I *feel* her come, feel the orgasm tighten her body, clenching around me like a vise, her lips fluttering against the rigid length of my cock as she arches her back, crying out with a sound that's almost a scream. My deep, guttural groan joins it as I feel myself start to come too, the first hot spurt of it so good that I feel as if I might pass out from the sheer pleasure of it. My vision darkens at the edges as I pitch forward, my mouth buried against her neck as I bury myself in her to the hilt, feeling her legs wrap around me, her breasts pressing against me. The orgasm feels as if it will never stop, my cock pulsing again and again as I empty myself into her.

When I roll off of her, panting and sweaty, I almost expect her to get up and leave. But instead, she rolls onto her side, propping her chin on her hand as she looks at me.

"I'm glad we're doing this again," she says softly. "I missed this."

That small alarm in the back of my head goes off again, but I choose to ignore it. The fog of need is gone, and usually, this is when my clarity returns, when I should be able to think straight again. But I still want her here. I think about what I promised, what feels like so long ago, to give her an apartment of her own and to live separately, and I can feel myself recoil at the thought.

I don't want her to leave anymore. I want—

I want whatever we almost had before. The thought is startling in its clarity. I've seen Sofia's strength now, her ability to handle the worst, her refusal to back down even from me. As much as her rebellion has angered me, I can see the backbone in her. She can be selfish and ungrateful, yes—but also tough. And after all, I've been all of those things, too.

What if we ruled this family together?

I was always supposed to be the bridge between Rossi and Franco's child, a son of Rossi's blood. I'd honored that because Rossi had been like my father, a man who had taken me in hand and finished raising me after my father died, my mentor as well as my boss. But now—

Now, after what he did to Sofia, I see things differently.

And I'm not so sure I want to keep the seat warm for his bloodline any longer.

Maybe, just maybe, we could make a dynasty of our own.

"I missed it too." I look over at her, at her flushed face, the hair at her forehead sticking there slightly. "I'll miss it while I'm gone, that's for sure."

Sofia frowns. "What? Where are you going?"

It occurs to me then that I didn't say anything to her about the conclave. I'm not entirely sure how much I can trust her yet, but I do know one thing—if I really do want to build something here, I'll have to talk to her like a husband does with his wife. I'll have to include her to let her know what's going on. It's both terrifying and invigorating to think about—the idea of having a partner at home, someone I can talk and share things with.

I've kept so much locked away for so long. I could share those things with Sofia—if it worked between us. And that thought is so new and confusing that it terrifies me.

I never been scared of much. But the thought of that kind of intimacy frightens me to my core.

And yet—there could be a kind of strength in it, too. To have one person who could have my back, no matter what. Who has no loyalties beyond our family and me and the future of our children.

I imagine Sofia holding a baby. *Our* baby. A son, I would hope. Loving him, caring for him. I imagine coming home to them both, and I don't recoil from the idea as I always have before. Instead, I feel an odd warmth. A feeling that is almost…hope.

"I've called a conclave of the families," I tell her, sitting up and pulling the sheet around my hips. "I'll be there, as well as Viktor and his second-in-command, and Colin and Liam Macgregor." I pause, realizing that she probably knows very little about how these things work. Her father kept her extremely sheltered from all of it. "Something like this is only called if there's a serious problem, if things have really gotten out of hand. The last one was a few decades ago when we had problems with the Irish. Rossi was a young man then." My expression grows serious as I look at her, frowning. "I mean to have peace, Sofia. I've made that clear. But whoever is responsible for our losses will pay. This conclave is meant to bring us into an agreement, to find out who is responsible and why, and what will settle the score so that we can move forward in harmony."

"Will you be safe?" Her mouth twists with worry, and I watch her face, wondering if it can all possibly be real. A few days ago, she was fighting with me, defending her reasons for running away. A few days ago, I was so furious with her that I slammed my hand into a mirror. But now, all I see is concern in her eyes—concern for me. And all I feel is the desire to make this work, to have a future that isn't as lonely as the one I'd reconciled myself to.

"I hope so. I should be. The etiquette is that there will be a cease-fire until the conclave happens, and peace is made or not. If we can't come to an agreement, then there will be war. But I hope it won't come to that," I add quickly. "And until then, there should be no more violence."

"How long until you leave?"

"A couple of weeks." I lean back, looking at her. I can't get enough of her face, of her sculpted cheekbones and dark eyes, the way her hair tumbles into her face when she moves. "Why?"

Sofia moves closer, her hand stroking over the ridges of my abdomen. "I thought maybe we could get away," she says hesitantly. "When things were good for a little while, you talked about us going on a honeymoon." Her voice speeds up then, her words tumbling over each other as if she's afraid I might interrupt her before she can finish. "We've had so many ups and downs, Luca. More downs than ups—but when it's been good...it's *good*. I thought maybe if we got away, if we went somewhere secluded and safe, that we could just be ourselves for a little while and see if this works without all of this." She waves her hand around the room. "If we actually *like* each other."

I consider that, watching her as I think. "And what if we don't?"

"Then, when the Bratva threat is gone like you said, you follow through on your promise and give me my own place. We live separate lives as much as we can. Or if you want, now that Rossi is dead, you can divorce me." Sofia's voice trembles the slightest bit at that, and I'm surprised at my own reaction to her words, too.

The thought of divorcing her makes me recoil instantly, thinking *no* with a violence that startles even me. *You're mine,* I think, and without thinking, I roll over, pinning her onto her back as I look down at her.

She gasps softly, and just that small sound has my cock hardening all over again.

"You want me to take you on a honeymoon?" I try to think rationally about it, if it's a good idea or not. I've told her no so many times before, but right this second—I'm having a very *hard* time.

"Please?" she whispers. "I—I want to try, Luca. Like we tried before."

Try as I might, I can't think of a reason not to. The cease-fire is in place, and I don't believe even Viktor will break it. He'd have the wrath of both the Irish and me down on him if he did—they'll stand behind me no matter what, but they won't want to get involved if it's just my beef with Viktor. I could call on them if it comes to war, and I probably will—but Colin will stay out of it as long as he can. And Viktor knows that—he won't want to give me a reason to force the Irish's hand or Colin a reason to come into the fray on his own. Those odds don't favor him.

As for everything else—Franco can handle the ordinary business operations and managing Ana while we're gone. In fact, it might be good for him to have that kind of responsibility, to give him something more to do than just stand in my shadow.

"Yes," I say, before I can change my mind or think of a reason to say no. "We'll do it. Let's go on a honeymoon."

This is the most ridiculous thing I've ever agreed to, I think as Sofia wraps her arms around my neck.

But as she pulls me down and my lips meet hers, I can't quite bring myself to care.

LUCA

11

I knew there was something wrong. I knew it.

The thought beats inside of my head, over and over again, as I sit in the back of my car, being driven to St. Patrick's to see Father Donahue. I don't know how happy the priest will be to see me after I decked him hard enough to knock him out not all that long ago, but he's the only person I can think of right now who I can talk to.

The only one who has to keep my secrets and who might be able to give me counsel. Because right now, my head is spinning, and I don't have the first idea what to do.

Two days ago, Sofia was in the middle of packing when she suddenly fled into the bathroom. I heard her throwing up just seconds later, despite the sound of the faucet running that she'd turned on to try to hide it. I hadn't thought much of it—there was any number of reasons why she might have been nauseous. Food that didn't sit well, a stomach bug—plenty of others.

Lots of reasons that didn't have anything to do with the fact that several weeks ago, we had a wild night of sex without using condoms—over and over again.

I'd pushed that thought out of my head, though. Until I heard Sofia get up in the middle of the night to vomit again. And then disappear during breakfast. And dinner. She was a little paler than normal, a little more tired, but other than that, she seemed fine. No lying in bed like she had food poisoning or the flu. No asking for someone to go out for medicine for her or having it sent to the apartment.

It made that alarm bell in the back of my head grow louder. And louder still.

And then I remembered that she'd gone to the hospital after I'd rescued her from the safe house.

I'd gone straight there, my stomach tying itself in knots with apprehension—the same feeling I have right now. I'd tracked down the nurse who had been in charge of Sofia while she was there. When she refused to budge when it came to telling me the truth about Sofia's medical records, I talked to her supervisor, who was very aware both of who I am and how much money I regularly pour into charitable donations to the hospital. I don't flex that particular muscle as often as Rossi used to—but in this case, I was more than happy to.

And it led to one very important piece of information.

Sofia is pregnant.

Not just pregnant—but actively trying to hide it from me.

It hit me like a punch to the gut—and I'd know what that feels like. I've had it happen plenty of times before, but physically, not metaphorically. Still, it felt as if all the wind had been taken out of me when I heard those words come out of that older, grey-haired lady's mouth.

"We had to test her before we could administer certain medications or take her for x rays—and it came back positive, beyond a doubt. Your wife is pregnant, but she was very insistent that she be the one to tell you herself."

For once, I hadn't flown into a rage. I'd been too shocked—and for another, I'd managed to hold back my fury at being lied to just long enough to consider why Sofia would keep something like that a secret from me.

The contract.

I'd made her sign it, and she'd agreed, believing then that we'd never sleep together. Certainly believing, as I had, that even if we did, we wouldn't want to more than once to seal the deal and satisfy my curiosity. Believing that we'd never develop feelings for one another, that our only feeling would be a deep, certain desire to live as separately as we possibly could.

There had been no desperate, passionate night in our future that we could see. No rooftop dates or sex in as many rooms of the house as we could manage. There was no frantic coupling after she caught me jerking off, too lost in the pleasure to rationally think about what could happen.

To her, then, I'm sure it seemed impossible that she could ever have to make that choice. And I'd been so certain of the path that I'd been set on, happy in my bachelorhood, satisfied with never being a father, content to hold the position until Franco's child could one day take it over, as we'd all agreed.

But now everything has changed.

Now I want my wife. I want her at my side, to cultivate that strength in her, to make us a force to be reckoned with. I want her in my bed, mine, so completely bound to me that no one will ever take her away. I want her safe, and our child—

I want our child alive and healthy. Able to inherit the dynasty that I'm desperately trying to secure during this conclave.

With this news, that possibility that had crept into my mind in bed with Sofia, the possibility of a mafia ruled by the Romano line and not the Rossi, has the potential to become a reality.

Your wife is pregnant.

Of course, she doesn't know that I've been thinking any of this. So as far as she knows, I'll want her to terminate the pregnancy immediately. And if she hasn't told me—that means she wants the baby, too.

But *does she want me, too?*

Her actions lately would say that she does. But I'm not sure how much of that was real and how much of it was just to throw me off until she could figure out what to do about the baby.

Was that why she tried to run?

Even if Father Donahue doesn't tell me the whole truth, I know that I have to talk to him. I need some clarity about what to do next.

Because I've never felt so lost.

As much as I miss my father, I haven't often felt the loss of him as keenly as I do now. I missed our friendship more than his advice—I'd had Rossi for that, to mentor and counsel me. But now I have neither, and right now, I would give anything to have my father sitting here, to tell me what I ought to do and to answer the question foremost in my mind.

What about Franco?

Far from being happy for us, I know he'll be furious at the news. He's counting on his child with Caterina taking over when I'm gone, on establishing a dynasty of his own. The idea of being usurped won't sit well with him, especially not with the current tension between us.

Not that he'd care, either, but I don't think Caterina would be quite as angry about it. In fact, I think she's more likely to be glad that her child wouldn't be the one to inherit all of this, especially considering that it's taken both her mother and father from her.

I think back to when I spoke with Caterina in the hospital and how she'd said she wanted peace because she and Franco were already trying for a baby. She could be pregnant already, and I know if that's the case, it'll be even harder to keep Franco from coming off the rails when he finds out that Sofia is pregnant.

I'm not sure what my options are. I could step down and give the seat to Franco, letting him start his reign now instead of vicariously through his child one day. But every part of me rebels at that idea. I was pushed into this role, but after all I've done, all I've suffered, all the pieces of my soul that I've sold to get and keep it, I feel that I've earned my place.

And the idea of passing it on to a child of my blood, instead of letting my legacy die with me, is suddenly intoxicating.

But first, Sofia has to trust me.

I walk into the church and see Father Donahue in one of the front pews. There's a scar on the back of his head, and when he turns

M. JAMES

around to look at me as I walk down the aisle, I can see one on his forehead as well.

Thankfully, me punching him in the jaw doesn't seem to have left any lasting damage.

"Father." I dip my head respectfully. "If I could have a little of your time?"

"As long as it isn't to go another round, aye. Of course." His Irish accent sounds a little thicker today, and it's a reminder that Father Donahue isn't one of us, not a part of the Italians that run this city. Some days that's a cause for concern, but today it's a relief. He has no vested interest in this beyond counseling me.

"I'm sorry for decking you." I make sure that he can hear the apology in my voice, because I mean it. "It was rash of me."

"You were in a bad place. I can understand that." The priest motions to the pew. "Come, Luca, sit down. Tell me what's on your mind. I can tell that something's pressing on you."

I don't beat around the bush. The moment we're seated, Father Donahue looking at me expectantly, I blurt it out.

"Sofia's pregnant."

The look of surprise on the priest's face isn't *quite* genuine enough to fool me. "Luca—"

I hold up a hand. "Don't bother breaking your vows to lie to me by saying you didn't know. Don't worry, I'm not going to ask you to share what Sofia told you or didn't tell you that night. But it makes more sense to me now why she ran and why she came to you for sanctuary."

Father Donahue nods. "So you know, then. Will you be making her stick to the terms of the agreement you both made?"

"That's what I'm here to talk to you about."

The priest hesitates. "Luca, I'm a priest of the Catholic church. You know what my answer will always be. I'll never encourage the ending of a pregnancy—"

"I know." I cut him off abruptly. "I want Sofia to keep the baby."

"You'll be pleased to know that she's agreeable to that. As to keeping the marriage along with the baby—" Father Donahue frowns.

"I didn't get the impression that all was well between you. But I would frown on divorce, as well. So my counsel, Luca, is going to be that you look to both your marriage and your future child, and decide how best to provide for and nurture both." He sighs heavily. "I know that happy marriages are not something that men like you put great stock in, but—"

"You're wrong about that, too," I interrupt. "Well, not entirely. I'll agree that we're raised to believe that our wives' happiness is not high on the list of priorities. But I also know that Sofia has always expected more than that out of a real marriage. Her parents had a marriage like that—good, loving. If I were to be a real husband to her, I would want to be a good one."

"A loving one?"

"I'm not sure love is a word that I'm familiar with," I confess. "I have feelings for Sofia, but—"

"Tell me this, Luca," Father Donahue says quietly. "That night when you went after her, were you concerned for your own life?"

"No, but—"

"When you married her, was it for her sake or yours?"

"Hers, but—"

The priest folds his hands in his lap, looking at me intently. "You believe that you're not capable of love, but your actions towards Sofia, while not always strictly those of a loving husband, show that you care deeply for her. That you are willing to put your own life in danger in order to save hers. That when she is threatened, you don't stop to think about the cost to yourself. That, Luca, is love. A type of it, anyway. And it can grow into more if you allow it."

"If I love her, she can very easily be used against me," I say quietly. "My enemies will know that she is the key to causing me to make rash, reckless decisions. What I did when I went to the safe house—that was rash and reckless."

"Vitto Rossi had an ocean of blood on his hands," Father Donahue says grimly. "His death was not undeserved. And if it came at your hands, if he was the one responsible for Sofia's kidnapping, then you did what you had to for your family. That, too, is love."

I narrow my eyes. "That's very perceptive of you, Father, to guess at that sequence of events."

He shrugs. "I've been a priest here for a very long time, Luca. I've seen the rise of the Rossi family, and I can't say that I was sorry to see it fall."

"That's the thing." I frown. "Franco's child is meant to inherit after me. That's why Rossi had him marry Caterina, so that his blood would continue on in some way. So that the family would continue to be run by his legacy. If Sofia is pregnant, that changes everything."

"And do you want it to change?"

"I don't know," I start to say, but even as the words come out of my mouth, I know they're wrong. "Yes," I say finally. "I do. I've bled, and killed, and tortured for the mafia. I've sinned a thousand times upon a thousand upon another thousand. I know there is no absolution for me, and I did it all because my father did it before me. After all, I was born into this life, and I know no other way. I was willing to let the title pass on to Rossi's blood because he was like a father to me. I only inherited the title because he had no son and because I didn't think I would ever have or want a wife. I was happy with my life the way it was. I was—"

I break off, realizing how much I've said. And there's more still to say.

"I thought I was happy. I never dreamed of a marriage or a child. But now, Sofia has made me wonder what it would be like if *we* were happy. Together. And the thought of a child to carry on my legacy, of making my own dynasty, of making everything that I've done part of something *worthwhile*, rather than just in the service of a man who turned out to be a sick, traitorous bastard—" I swallow hard, my hands clenching into fists.

"I killed Vitto Rossi, Father," I say defiantly, looking at him. "I know there is no absolution for that. But he tortured my wife. He would have had her raped, killed, violated a dozen ways before he let her die. I feel no guilt for killing him, no sorrow. But—he was all the father I had left. I've lost my mother, my father twice over, and I have no one left. Except—"

"Sofia." Father Donahue's voice is quiet.

"If she'll have me. But after everything I've done to her—after everything we've done to each other, I don't know how to trust this. I don't know how to love. I don't know how to be a father."

"Be like yours." The priest looks at me. "Matteo Romano had faults, Luca, but deep down, he was a good man. Better than Vitto Rossi. He made a promise to Sofia's father, and you've followed through on it. If you want my opinion—" he hesitates, looking me full in the eyes. "The Romano bloodline deserves to rule more than the Rossi line."

"And my sin? Killing Vitto? You must judge me for that, surely—"

"It's not my place to judge you," Father Donahue says quietly. "Nor can I give you absolution, as you well know. But if you are asking me as a man, and not as a priest...you did well, Luca. Vitto Rossi was a violent man, a bloodthirsty one. I know that you can be every bit as ruthless. But when you are, it's for a reason."

He leans forward then, his gaze intent. "I will not tell you to be a different man, Luca. Be ruthless. But be ruthless in the pursuit of your wife, of safety for your family, for your child. Be ruthless in protecting the things that you can love and that will love you in return. If you do this, you can build a legacy that will last generations. It's not weak to love, Luca. In fact, I believe that love will make you stronger than you were before. *She* can make you stronger if you treat her with the respect and honor that you vowed to at the altar."

"What do you know of love?" I can hear the challenge in my voice, and Father Donahue smiles.

"Of love between a man and a woman, nothing. But I love God. I love this church and its congregation. And I love this city, Luca. I wish nothing more for there to be peace in her streets instead of blood. I loved your father and Sofia's. I witnessed the vows they made, as I witnessed the ones you made to Giovanni's daughter. And I will say one last thing to you, Luca. If you take nothing else to heart, heed this."

He pauses, and I can feel the silence of the church around us, weighing down the air.

"Keep the promise, Luca. The one your father made, and the one you made. Keep it, and all will be well."

His words haunt me long after I leave. Long after I've gone home and gone about my night, and on and on until I lay in the darkness next to Sofia, knowing that now we both have a secret that we're keeping from each other. The same secret that we both know.

She hasn't told me, and I haven't told her.

And I won't until I'm sure of what to do next. Until I'm sure of her feelings and mine. And suddenly, looking at her sleeping face in the darkness, I'm very glad that I agreed to this ridiculous honeymoon.

Keep the promise, Luca.

SOFIA

12

From the moment we step onto Luca's private jet to leave on the honeymoon, I feel as if I've been transported into a different world.

I've never been on a private jet before, and it's exactly as luxurious as I would have imagined. Luca looks as if he was made for it, lounging back comfortably in one of the buttery leather seats. I rarely see him dressed casually, it's always suits and ties, but today he's wearing Armani jeans and a soft charcoal grey V-neck that makes me want to run my hands over his chest even more than usual. His dark hair is swept away from his face with less product than usual, making it look slightly messy as if he's just run his hands through it, and he seems—more relaxed than usual? I can't quite put my finger on what it is, but he seems different.

For one thing, he's more affectionate. I don't know if he's just playing the part of the doting newlywed husband leaving on his honeymoon. Still, as I walk up the steps ahead of him, I feel his hand on the small of my back, drifting to my hip as we walk down the aisle of the plane towards our seats. There's already champagne set out, and my stomach twists as I see the two glasses. *Fuck*. I hadn't thought about how I was going to explain away not drinking. Luca knows very well that I enjoy drinking champagne—or wine, or gin, or margaritas.

Well, shit. That makes me sound like I have an alcohol problem.

I guess I could play it off as saying that I'm cutting back, but I'm not sure he'll believe me. I could say that I'm not feeling well, which is at least partially true—I've been throwing up more than I'd ever been led to believe I would while pregnant.

"Morning" sickness is apparently not just in the morning. I feel lied to every few hours these days.

Still, I don't want to fake sick during the times that I'm actually feeling okay. Which leaves me with the resolution that all I can do is just get through it one refused drink at a time and figure it out as I go.

At least for this first glass, it's easy.

"To our belated honeymoon," Luca says with a smile once we're in our seats and the pilot is readying for takeoff, tapping the glass against mine. "My lovely wife."

"I can't wait." I smile at him, and it's not hard to do. It's too easy, in fact, when I'm supposed to be faking this. Plotting my escape, waiting on Ana's information. But instead, I'm legitimately excited for this trip. Excited to find out where he's taking me. For once, I'm not afraid or worried. "You could have told me our destination," I tease him lightly, hoping to distract him from the fact that I'm not actually drinking the champagne.

"I like to surprise you every once in a while," he says with a grin. "I promise you'll like it." He glances at my champagne flute, and my heart sinks a little. "You don't like it? It's the same one that was served at our wedding. I thought it would be romantic."

"It is," I assure him, and—it *really* is. I'm surprised that he would have even thought of such a thing, and it makes me pause for a moment, looking at him curiously. "Did you really know that? Did someone suggest that you have that on the flight?"

Luca smirks. "Sofia, I know you don't think all that highly of me, but I'm not just a cold, heartless killer. I did notice what champagne was served at our wedding, and it *was* my idea to have it on the flight." He pauses. "I *am* trying, Sofia."

The strange thing is, I really believe him. I look at his face, and everything about it seems sincere. I've seen Luca angry, hiding things from me, evasive and cold. He's none of those things right now. He looks for all the world like a husband trying to make things right with his wife.

What if he's pretending like I am? What if we're both playing a game with each other?

The problem with all of this, with all the promises we've broken and lies we've told, with the secret I'm keeping right now and the game I'm playing, is that I'm not sure I can trust him any more than I know he can trust me.

And if neither of us can trust each other, we'll never have a happy marriage.

Is that what you think this might be? A happy marriage?

I don't know what to think anymore. I don't even know what I want. I—

My train of thought is interrupted by my stomach twisting. I nearly heave into Luca's lap before I'm able to make a beeline to the toilet, which is arguably nicer than any plane bathroom that I've ever experienced before. Not that I've flown very often.

Luca raises an eyebrow when I return to my seat. "Not feeling well?"

"I think I get a little airsick." It might actually be part of it—now that the plane has evened out, I think I feel alright, but the ascent and the brief turn that we did nauseated me in a way that I'm pretty sure had nothing to do with my pregnancy and everything to do with climbing 36,000 feet up in the air.

I wish we could just teleport to our destination.

Fortunately, Luca seems happy to accept that as an excuse for why I'm not drinking my champagne. We settle into our seats, and he reaches into a compartment and hands me a soft beige cashmere blanket. "In case you get cold," he says, and I blink at him, momentarily startled by the thoughtfulness of the gesture.

I want to ask him what's going on, why he's behaving like this, but I'm almost afraid to. I *like* it, but I don't know what to do with it. Luca has never been kind or gentle. Even in bed, he's rough and filthy and passionate, and I like it that way. I've wondered from time to time what it would be like if we "made love," if we had slow, sensual, romantic sex, what it would feel like for him to kiss me gently, with love instead of hot, fiery rage mixed with passion.

I can't even imagine it, honestly. And I don't know how to feel about this change in Luca because I don't understand it.

We don't talk much for the rest of the flight. Luca has a book with him—something else that I've never seen, at home when I have shared a bed with him, we've usually had sex until we fall asleep, or I'm asleep long before he comes home. I do too, and we pass the majority of the flight in companionable silence. It feels intimate and domestic, and I can feel myself relaxing into it, allowing myself to be lulled by the simple pleasure of reading side by side on a plane.

A private plane headed to some unknown exotic location, I remind myself. We're not some average couple on our way to Disneyland. We never will be.

But is that what you want? Stealing a sideways glance at Luca, who is absorbed in his book—some science-fiction drama, if I can judge the book by its cover—I wonder if that's really what I would want. I never really dated before Luca, never thought about what I would want in a husband because I'd never expected to have one. Marriage hadn't been something I even considered. Would I want to be sitting on a commercial flight right now, next to a man with a dad bod and the latest James Patterson, wearing cargo shorts and New Balances while we flew with our screaming kids to Orlando?

Or, for all my protestations and complaints, is this what I actually want? A husband who is bloody and deadly, to be sure, but who is also violently protective of me, even if to a fault? A husband who has proven that he will literally kill to keep me safe, who is facing down the Bratva for me, who faced down his own boss even to the death to keep me alive? Who married me even though he didn't want a wife? Who has shown that even if he can be possessive and mercurial and even a little bit controlling, will stop at nothing to make sure that no one harms me?

Not to mention a husband who is gorgeous, over six feet of chiseled, rock-hard muscle, with a cock that makes me blush just thinking about it and talents in bed that I never imagined. A husband who wants to fuck me, use me, make me his in every filthy way he can, and who knows how to play my body like the violin that I haven't touched in so long.

A husband who I know that, for a little while at least, I was falling in love with.

I think I could still love him. If I could trust him. And most importantly, if I knew I could trust him with our baby.

The urge to touch my stomach is too strong to resist, and I slide my hand under the soft blanket, feeling my still-flat belly under my Lululemon leggings. If Luca sees, I'll just pass it off as nausea, but the touch is reassuring, even if there's nothing there to actually feel yet.

I have to get out before I start to show. But looking at Luca as he reads his book, his brow furrowed at some particularly interesting passage, I can feel my heart beginning to ache. I don't know if that's what I really want, and for the first time, I wish I hadn't gotten pregnant just yet. I wish I had more time to figure this out. To decide.

Maybe this honeymoon was a bad idea.

* * *

I MANAGE to only throw up once more, which is a record for me lately. But as the plane starts to descend, I look out of the window and forget all about my roiling stomach.

Underneath us is the bluest water I've ever seen, stretching out for miles all around in shades of turquoise and teal that I never knew existed in real life. I can see beaches in the distance, and I can see scattered buildings below, as well as what looks like a large hotel further off.

"Where are we?" I ask, glancing at Luca with my mouth agape, struggling to take in the beauty of it all.

He grins, clearly enjoying my reaction. "Welcome to our honeymoon, darling. We're in Mustique."

SOFIA

MUSTIQUE.

13

I've heard of it, obviously. It's a celebrity playground, where the Duke and Duchess of Cambridge went for *their* honeymoon—and now where I'm spending mine. It feels a little like something out of a fairy tale, something I'd never even imagined. I've already gone from wondering if this was actually a good idea to being incredibly glad that I suggested to Luca that we go.

But even more overwhelming is that he chose the destination. And he picked *this*. It's romantic beyond belief, a private island with only a small amount of other visitors. Or so I think, until Luca takes my hand, his smile spreading even wider across his face.

"I bought out every villa on the entire island for the week," he says, grinning at me. "This private island is entirely ours, without another soul on it, except for the staff. We can take our pick of places to stay. For the next week, Mustique is ours."

I can't even imagine how much that must have cost. And more than that, looking at Luca, I don't think he did this just out of fear of someone harming me or because he's so jealous that he doesn't want to risk some strange man catching a glimpse of me in a bikini.

He did this to be romantic. He did this for *me* as a grand gesture.

It's almost like he's trying to make everything bad that's happened between us so far up to me.

The air is warm and humid as we step off of the plane, and I can feel my hair frizzing slightly, blowing in the floral-scented breeze as we walk out onto the tarmac. A smile spreads across my face, and I know that there's no way I'm going to be able to *not* do exactly what I'd asked Luca here to do.

To spend time with each other, away from everything. To try to understand each other better, and if we could be happy.

Maybe by the end of this, I'll know if I can trust him with my secret. If I can stop playing these games and just be his wife.

The thought of it sounds too unfathomable to be true.

Luca points out the villas as we ride towards them, noting different things that make them stand out. "That one has an infinity pool," he says, "and that one is more of a rustic style, that one is set off of the beach a ways. But that one has a pool that leads right into the water. It's basically an island in and of itself."

"That one," I say immediately. It sounds like exactly what I want, an island on an island, a place so secluded that I can't do anything other than pretend the outside world doesn't exist.

"Are you sure?" Luca grins. "You haven't seen the interiors."

"I'm sure," I tell him firmly, and I feel his hand slide into mine again as we walk towards the entrance of the villa.

I'm immediately happy with my choice. We're on a tropical, beautiful island, in an exotic and faraway place, completely isolated from the rest of the world. Yet, this villa makes it feel even more so. "This one was designed by a famous Mexican architect," Luca tells me as we walk, and I look around wide-eyed, taking it all in.

It's astounding, from the tiled stonework along the path as we walk in, to the manicured-yet-wild landscape of shrubs, fronds, vines, flowers, and palm trees, to the roughly hewn stone walls. The villa itself has grass and straw roofing over the terracotta and clay-like walls, and I see the infinity pool Luca talked about, the edge of it stretching up to the gorgeous turquoise blue waters. The deck has multiple spaces for lounging, with potted trees and plants and a magnificent macrame hammock hanging just by the water. There's a massive rock fireplace, made out of boulder-sized stones, pieced together in a way that looks wholly natural as if they just happened to exist in an arrangement that's perfect for building a fire in. Everything looks slightly untamed, just a little primitive, and very exotic while still being more luxurious than even Luca's penthouse back home.

We haven't even been inside, and I'm already in love with it. Luca's place is gorgeous, but it's never felt comfortable. This feels just rustic enough, somewhere that I can actually relax, despite the fact that it's probably insanely expensive.

"Can we stay here forever?" I say as I look over at Luca, only half-joking. *God, if only we could.* I imagine the two of us—eventually three—on this private island forever, far away from mafias and mobs and Bratva, bosses and underbosses, Italians and Russians and Irish and all the conflicts that have gone on for years upon years upon years. It sounds like a paradise.

It sounds like a heaven I've never dared to imagine. At that moment, looking at my husband's happy, relaxed face so far away from everything that's plagued us, I'm sure of one thing.

It's not Luca that I hate. It's the man that the mafia makes him into. It's the other side of him, the Jekyll to his Hyde. The man that comes out when he feels threatened or trapped or angry.

That man terrifies me.

The man standing next to me now, holding my hand as we look around the villa where we're going to be living for the next week—he's the man I could love.

"Wouldn't that be nice," Luca says, and I think I hear genuine wistfulness in his voice.

"Is this your first time here?"

"No." Luca glances at me. "And before you ask, no, I've never brought a woman here before. I've barely even spent the night with one before you, remember?"

I do remember. It's part of what's so hard to reconcile about the two different sides of Luca. That the playboy who kicked every woman out of his bed seconds after he came has not only let me sleep next to him for more nights than I have fingers to count on now, but actually *ordered* me to.

I'm the first woman that he can't seem to get enough of, and there's a heady power in that.

The interior of the villa is as gorgeous as the outside. The floors are cool white and beige stone, overlaid with woven rugs. Everything looks beautifully natural—the beds made from exotic-looking wood, the white linen sheets, the heavy oatmeal-colored drapes at the windows, stirring in the breeze. The bathroom is huge, all stone and blue glass and white tiles, with a shower to rival the one back at Luca's penthouse and wicker baskets holding towels and washcloths.

"The villa comes with its own staff," Luca explains. "There's a housekeeper, maids, and a butler, as well as a concierge if we need anything. We won't have to leave the villa for a single thing if we don't want to." He smiles when he says that, and a shiver of desire runs down my spine as I realize how close we are to the bed.

I expect him to say dirty things to me, to order me to my knees, to strip me bare and tease me until I'm begging. But instead, Luca surprises me for what feels like the hundredth time already today.

His hand slides over my cheek, his palm warm and gentle against my skin. His eyes lock with mine, and I have that same dizzying feeling that I've had before with him, as if the room has narrowed down to the two of us, everything else blurring out and drifting away. I can't imagine anyone else ever making me feel like this, as if we're the only two people in the world—and right now, here on this island, we all but are.

When his lips come down on mine, it's not hard and passionate. It's soft and gentle, his mouth brushing over mine as if he's kissing me for the first time. His other hand slides up my waist, bunching in the soft fabric of my t-shirt, and I gasp, arching towards him without thinking as I feel the stirring of desire in my blood.

But it's slow and sweet this time, not hot and furious. This isn't hate mixed with lust, anger mixed with desire; it's just the need of two people for each other, our bodies moving into one another as if we have no other choice. His mouth never leaves mine as he strips away my shirt and then my leggings, as my hands take off his clothing piece by piece until we fall naked together on the cool linen sheets of the bed.

Outside I can hear the waves faintly lapping at the shore, the rustling of the breeze in palm fronds, and I feel my heart aching as Luca trails his lips down my neck. His breath comes short and quick, his nose brushing over my skin as he caresses my breasts, my waist, my hips, his body rubbing against mine in the sweet, slow way that I'd always imagined two people come together.

"Sofia—" he whispers my name, his eyes meeting mine, and I see something there that I never have before. There's a naked rawness in his gaze, a need that's different from anything before. I respond without thinking to it, wrapping my arms around his neck as I arch up against him, whimpering slightly at the sensation of my nipples rubbing against his hard chest.

I feel him pressing between my legs, hard and thick. I let my legs fall open for him, wrapping them around his waist as I feel his hips push forward, the first inch of him sinking into me and making me cry out with pleasure. I expect him to start thrusting then, fast and powerful, but he doesn't.

He keeps that same slow pace, stroking in and out of me with long, steady thrusts that feel better than anything we've done before, better than the teasing, better than the rough sex. It feels different, charged with an emotion that we haven't shared before. As I wrap myself around him, feeling my orgasm building, I know that we're hovering on the precipice of something.

I know that this is dangerous. Because I could lose myself so much more easily now than ever before.

Before I know it, the afternoon is fading away into the evening, and we're still lying on the now-messy linen sheets, the humid air turning cooler as the breeze picks up.

"I'm hungry," Luca murmurs, rolling to face me. "I think we should order dinner."

"Okay." My voice is a whisper, and I feel as if I'm still trying to process all of this. This is the first time Luca and I have ever spent an entire day together, the first time we've ever done something so simple as read next to each other. The first time we've flown somewhere together, gone on vacation, and definitely the first time we've done—whatever I should call what we've been doing for the past few hours.

If it were with anyone else, I'd say we'd been making love. But beyond the ridiculous cheesiness of the term, that's not something I've ever been able to imagine Luca doing—or us doing together.

"We can ask for something specific," Luca continues, completely oblivious to my mental turmoil, "but the villa comes with a private chef. I'd recommend we let him bring us whatever he decides to make."

"That sounds fine to me." I smile at him, trying to hide my nerves. *Surely there's something else to this, right? Surely this is a trick. A way to get me to let my guard down.*

If it is, then it's working.

We shower first, taking turns beneath the water. At one point, I feel Luca's hand drifting down my spine, trailing over my skin in a way that makes me shiver deliciously. He seems to want to touch me, to feel me, almost as if he's afraid I might disappear. It makes me wonder what he's thinking, but as always, that's still very much a mystery.

I change into a light, fluttery blue patterned sundress with flat leather sandals and gold filigree jewelry for dinner, leaving my hair loose around my shoulders. The air-drying and humidity has given it a soft wave, and I can see Luca looking at me appreciatively as we walk out onto the balcony where our table is already set, a bottle of white wine chilling in an ice bucket.

Fuck. I should start counting how many times I'm going to have to dodge alcohol this week.

Luca pulls out the chair for me, and I look up at him, trying to see him not as the husband that I've had such a strange, off-and-on relationship with, but just as a man. A man who has gone to some lengths to plan a romantic vacation for us, a man that I just had sweet, loving sex with, and now a man who is doing things for me like pulling out a chair. A handsome, charming, charismatic man who could, in theory, be all mine forever.

Luca uncorks the bottle, sniffing it lightly before pouring us each a glass. "To our first night on our own island," he says, tapping the glass against mine, and I smile before lifting it to my lips and tasting it just a little.

Doctors say half a glass is fine, right? The first tiny sip makes me wish I could drink as much as I want. It's crisp and refreshing and fruity, with flavors of apple and pear and vanilla that are beyond any grocery store chardonnay I've ever bought. I set the glass down with some regret, looking over at Luca as a member of the staff brings out our salads, something with microgreens and finely shaved cheese and slivered pineapple, with a lemony vinaigrette.

"This is incredible," Luca says after the first bite. "All of this is. It's been a long time since I've been on a vacation."

"Really?" I look over at him, surprised. With as much money as he has, I would have thought he'd be vacationing all the time. "When was the last time you went on a vacation?"

Luca makes a face. "About three years ago, I think, to Ibiza. Not a vacation you'd want to hear about, though," he adds.

"Oh." I try to picture the kind of trip he's talking about—probably one with a lot of supermodels, illegal substances, and other things that I have absolutely no experience with. I blurt out my next question before I can stop myself. "Does it bother you that I'm not very—I guess 'worldly' would be the term? That I'm just…sheltered, I guess?"

"No," Luca says flatly. "Not a bit. I suppose someone who was raised to be a part of the mafia life, rather than being sheltered from it, would have been helpful. But it's not something you could help. And I don't blame your father for wanting you out of this life."

Even that short statement is enough to give me a tiny flare of hope. I know I'm reaching, grasping at straws, but I want something. Something that could mean that this week isn't just a flicker of happiness before I have to snuff out the ember of whatever could be between us.

"What if you had a child?" I ask tentatively. I *know* this is brushing too close to danger, too close to telling him the truth, but I can't help it. "Would you want them to be part of this?"

Luca pauses, setting down his fork as he looks at me, and there's an expression in his eyes that I can't quite read. But he's serious when he answers. He doesn't brush me off or remind me about the contract I signed, that he's never *supposed* to have a child.

"Well," he says slowly. "I know you want me to say no, that I wouldn't want them raised in this kind of life. But the answer is more complicated than that." He grins. "You ask me some challenging questions sometimes, Sofia. Like the one about what kind of husband I would want to be. Now you're asking me what kind of father."

"Is that a bad thing?" My voice drops slightly, hushed. My salad is forgotten in front of me; all I can think about are Luca's eyes, fixed on mine, his expression sincere and thoughtful. This is the different Luca, the one who cares. The one who listens to me.

"No." Luca shakes his head. "I like that you challenge me sometimes. Other times it can be infuriating," he says with a smirk. "But I don't think I'd be so attracted to you if you were like other women, just rolling over and spreading your legs for me, fawning over me. Or if you were a doormat, someone who cried all the time, who just gave in to things you didn't want without a fight. There's a fire in you, Sofia, and despite myself—I like that."

It's all I can do to keep my mouth from dropping open. It's not something I'd ever thought I'd hear him say to me.

"As far as a child—" Luca hesitates. "If I had a son, I'd want him to take over after me. To continue the legacy that I'd built. To make all of this worth it somehow. And a daughter—" he pauses, looking at me with that intense green gaze.

"Six months ago, even, I would probably have had a different answer for that. But after seeing what you've been through and what Caterina's been through—I would raise a daughter differently. I wouldn't sell her off in marriage to make an alliance. I've seen the pain that can cause all too closely now."

"And what about if you only had a daughter and not a son?" I watch his face, knowing I should steer the conversation away from this, but I'm too damn curious. "What then?"

"It's never been the way of the mafia to have a daughter inherit," Luca says carefully. "But—ways of doing things can change."

That, more than anything else, startles me.

"What about people?" I ask softly. "Do you think they can change?"

"If they want to."

The sentence hangs in the air between us. I can hear my heart beating, each pulse punctuating the silence, and I know that I want this. I want us. I want the man sitting in front of me because I believe this man wouldn't tell me to get rid of the child we made together the night that we both truly wanted each other for the first time.

"Luca, I—"

He leans towards me, capturing my face in his hands as the breeze ruffles my hair, and I breathe in as he kisses me. I can smell the salt on the air, and the fruity waft of the wine, the spice of his cologne, and the warmth of his skin, and I want him. My body feels liquified, melting, as boneless and warm as the wax in the votive candles on the table.

I want to stay here forever. I never want this to end.

A thunderclap breaks us apart, and before we can even make a move to look around or get up or check the weather, the skies open, and it starts to pour.

Luca grabs my hand, helping me out of my chair as we run back into the villa, already drenched and both of us laughing. Outside, the rain is pouring in sheets, lighting splitting the sky, the table and wine and our food all completely soaked in the storm that came out of nowhere.

"It's like that out here," Luca says with a laugh. "Beautiful one minute and raining the next."

I turn towards him, my heart pounding in my chest as I look up at his gorgeous, chiseled face. "Kind of like us."

His gaze searches mine, and I don't know what he's looking for there or if he's found it. All I know is that when he kisses me, there's no thought of resistance in me. Not when his tongue slides hotly into my mouth, his hands tangling in my wet hair as he pulls me up tightly against him, and not when we wind up on the cool stone tile together, the French doors still open and the curtains flapping wildly in the wind that picks up as the rain spills across the doorway.

We're already wet, though, and neither of us cares. My skirt winds up around my hips, Luca's jeans undone and shoved down, and in seconds he's inside of me. It's not soft and sweet like earlier, but it's not rough and angry either. It's something else altogether, his movements almost—desperate? It reminds me of the night he flew home after the intruder, the way he seemed to *need* me with a ferocity that went bone-deep, to remind himself that I was alive, that I was still his.

And I feel it too. We cling to each other, sopping wet, our skin burning with a feverish heat in the cold rainy evening. I forget where I end, and he begins as I tangle my legs with his, straining against each other.

It's as if we both know we're hovering on the knife's edge of losing one another, that we're at a crossroads. We've both made deals with the devil to get here, and now I know I have to pay the price.

I just hadn't thought I would lose my heart in the bargain.

SOFIA

14

We end up showering again afterward to warm up and then change into more comfortable clothes—soft cashmere joggers and a tight cropped tank top for me, grey sweatpants and a white t-shirt for Luca. I've rarely seen him like this, either. Usually, at home, he stays in his work clothes until it's time to go to bed, and to me, it's even hotter than anything else I've seen him in. He looks comfortable and relaxed, even his hair messier than normal, and it's so different from how he usually is. But then again, everything about this week is like that.

Almost as soon as we get out of the shower, the electricity goes out, the storm still raging outside. A few minutes later, there's a knock at the door—one of the staff come to see if we still want our dinner, and to apologize, even though there's clearly nothing about this that's anyone's fault.

The result is that we eat the rest of our dinner by candlelight in the dining room, which overlooks the water. We can see the entire storm outside of the glass doors, the lightning crackling again and again and the sheets of rain pouring down as we eat spiced roast duck and buttery mashed potatoes and crispy brussels sprouts fried with pancetta and orange and some kind of glaze that tastes better than I ever imagined brussels sprouts could.

I can't help thinking later, falling asleep to the sound of the slowing rain, that today must have been a fluke. A test, or something, that Luca dreamed up. Even when he pulls me into his arms to sleep, something he never does, I can't let myself fully relax into it.

But for the rest of the week, it doesn't change. We eat breakfast on the balcony the next morning, the sun as crisp and clear and blue as it was stormy the night before. It's delicious—poached eggs and smoked salmon and waffles with honey blossom and vanilla syrup dripping off of them along with melted butter. I want to eat every bite of it.

The result is that I make it halfway through the first heartbreakingly delicious waffle before I have to bolt into the bathroom to throw up.

When I come back out, Luca is looking at me strangely. "Are you okay?" is all he asks, spearing a piece of boar sausage, but I can hear something else in his voice. It makes me wonder if he's starting to suspect.

"Just leftover from the flight is all, I think," I say weakly, knowing how bad of an excuse it is. I've never heard of jet lag making anyone puke. But it's the best I can come up with under pressure.

I'm going to have to figure out a way to throw up more privately.

Fortunately, Luca doesn't question my decision to stick to water this morning as my drink. After breakfast, we change into our bathing suits. When I walk out onto the deck where Luca is already stretched out on a lounge chair, he catches sight of me and whistles so appreciatively that I know he's being serious.

"You've seen me naked before," I tease him, "and in lingerie. Surely me in a bikini isn't all that startling?"

"There's something that's just better about a gorgeous girl in a bikini," he informs me. "Go on, get in the pool. I want to see you in it all wet."

Before this, I might have complained or tried to argue, but instead, I just sway towards the sparkling infinity pool, enjoying the feeling of his eyes on me. I'd picked out an aqua blue string bikini for the occasion, one that ties on my hips and barely covers the curves of my ass, with a top that isn't really meant to constrain my full, C-cup breasts. There's some definite under and side-boob, and I can see when I turn around that Luca's already getting hard just watching me.

I dive into the cool water, swimming a few strokes and then standing up. A smile spreads across my face as I look at Luca; it feels impossible to be unhappy here, under the sun, in this beautiful water, with everything I could possibly want or need at my disposal and the most gorgeous man I've ever seen looking at me like I'm a goddess.

Everything back home feels so far away, as if it happened in another world, to different people. I know that's not true.

But it's so easy to pretend.

Luca's hand goes to the waist of his swim trunks. He's barely pulled out his hard cock before I'm walking towards him, my body already hungry for his all over again as I straddle the lounge chair, pushing my wet bikini aside and sliding down on top of him.

Here, I feel like someone else. Someone beautiful, wanton, seductive. Someone who can do something like this—walk sexily over to my husband and sit on his cock without feeling shy or embarrassed. And Luca fucking loves it. I can tell in the way he grabs my hips, the way he growls as he kisses me, the way he can't seem to get enough, his hands and mouth everywhere as he pulls me down to him while I ride his cock, on my neck and breasts and back up to my lips.

It's like that, every day. We have our meals on the balcony or the deck or in the dining room with the doors flung open to let in the sea breeze, one morning sitting just outside our bedroom and another by the pool, feeding each other bites of fruit and pieces of cheese under the island sunlight. We sunbathe by the pool and swim in the sea. Luca takes me snorkeling, pointing out different fish as they swim by, kissing me when we resurface. He takes me horseback riding on the beach, which neither of us has ever done before. For the first time, I see something actually approaching fear on Luca's face when his horse starts to snort and trot just a little bit too fast, ignoring him as he pulls back on the reins.

I can't help but laugh—Luca is this tough, alpha mafia boss, a man capable of so much violence and instilling so much fear in others. Still, atop the prancing black horse, he looks completely unsure of himself. It's endearing, in a way, to see him look so human, so—normal.

I lose track of how many times we make love—because that's what it feels like. There's no anger, no hate, no resentment; it's as if closing ourselves off from the rest of the world for a little while has made us forget about all of that. It's stripped us down, literally and figuratively, to just who we are as people—not Giovanni's daughter or Marco's son, not an orphaned violinist or a mafia don, not an unwilling bride or a reluctant groom.

Just Sofia and Luca.

And I find, over the course of the week, that I like who we are.

But of course, that only makes it all more complicated. Because I still have my secret, and he or she is growing by the day.

I almost tell Luca a few times. It's on the tip of my tongue, usually in our most intimate moments, but every time I stop myself. There's still that lingering fear that something about this isn't real, that the other shoe is going to drop at any moment. And then I think of Ana and what she might have learned, if she's found a way out for the baby and me, and I'm confused all over again.

I don't think I want a way out anymore.

But what if I'm wrong?

I feel on the verge of tears on the entire flight home. Luca and I made love one last time in the cool linen-sheeted bed before packing up to leave, and I clung to him, wishing I could stop time and not have to go back to reality.

To not have to make the choices that I will soon.

We're both quiet on the flight back. I wonder if Luca is feeling the same things I am, thinking the same things. I don't dare ask. I can feel the tension growing as the hour's tick by and we near home, and I feel a tight sickness in my stomach, one that has nothing to do with my pregnancy.

I don't want to go back to the way things were before. I can't regret the time we spent together on the honeymoon—it was one of the best weeks of my life—but it's so much harder now, knowing what we can be together. Knowing for sure how *good* we can be, that the brief space of time before this wasn't just a fluke.

This could be real. And I want it.

There's a car waiting for us on the tarmac. When we slide inside, I expect Luca to pull away, to shut down again, but he doesn't. Instead, he reaches for my hand, and I feel my chest squeeze tightly as his fingers lace through mine.

I wasn't sure what to expect once we got back to the penthouse, if we'd go back to being tense and cold to one another, if it would be awkward, if the last week would just disappear.

I never in my wildest dreams would have expected what we saw as the elevator doors opened.

There's blood smeared across the floor, the walls, a bloody handprint halfway up as if someone tried to catch themselves before they fell or pulled themselves to their feet. Luca flinches back immediately, his hand going for a gun that isn't there as he pushes me behind him forcefully, taking a few steps back and looking around.

"We'll take the stairs," he says decisively. "Stay behind me."

For once, I'm too freaked out to argue. I do exactly that, following him up the stairs. It's exhausting, going all the way up to the penthouse. By the time we reach our floor, I'm panting so hard that I'd almost have just rather ridden in the bloody elevator.

Luca carefully pushes the door open, listening for footsteps or noise for a moment. There's a faint, low groan, and he frowns.

"What the fuck?" he mutters, peering out into the hall. "Shit."

He says the last more loudly, swearing fervently, and my stomach clenches at the thought of what might be out there. I think of someone leaving us an injured animal as some kind of twisted warning or the half-alive body of one of Luca's men. And sure enough, when we both step out into the hall, there's a body crumpled at our doorstep. The hall carpet is streaked with blood, and as we carefully approach, I can see it all over the body, on the hands, the arms, the face—*her* face.

I clap my hands over my mouth, stifling a scream.
The body on our doorstep is Ana.

SOFIA

15

For a minute, I'm not even sure if she's alive. But then she moves, just slightly, and another groan comes from between her split and swollen lips.

"We need to get her inside," Luca says urgently. "Hurry! Help me with her."

She's dead weight, but somehow the two of us manage to carefully maneuver her inside and to the nearest guest bathroom on the first floor of the apartment. I'm impressed with how Luca doesn't seem to care that there's blood dripping all over the floor or that it's smeared on his jeans and new white t-shirt. He's laser-focused on us getting her somewhere that we can get a better look at her injuries. As we lay her down on the warm, heated tiles of the bathroom floor, Luca starts to run the taps in the bath.

"We need to warm her up, keep her from going into shock," he says firmly. "Sofia, is she responding at all?"

"A little, I think? We should take her to the hospital, call 911—"

"No." Luca's voice is firm. "We don't know how long ago this happened. If it was the Bratva, they could still be close. They could be waiting for us to do exactly that. We need to take care of her here, where it's safer."

RUTHLESS PROMISE

I don't argue with him. Instead, I turn my attention back to Ana, trying to take stock of her injuries. Her lips are swollen and purplish-red, her cheekbones battered and bruised, her eyes swollen almost shut. Her face is bloody, and a chunk of her hair is missing, her scalp bleeding where it was torn out.

"Check her mouth," Luca orders. "Her teeth."

Horror washes over me at the thought, making my stomach clench and turn over, but I force it down. *I'm not going to throw up now. I'm not!* Instead, wincing at the indignity of it, I pry her lips open, checking her teeth and the inside of her mouth for injuries. But her tongue and teeth are all fine, and from what I can tell, her nails are all intact as well. And then, as I scan down the length of her body, her clothes ripped and torn, I see something that makes me almost scream and choke back bile.

Her feet are purple, bruised, and beaten, and I can see crisscrossing cuts on the soles of her feet, deep gashes that are crusted with blood. Her large and pinky toes look broken, and I clap my hand over my mouth, trying not to burst into tears.

"Her feet, Luca—"

He glances back, and I see real horror on his face. It makes me feel even worse somehow because I know that Luca has done terrible things. He's tortured men, inflicted awful pain. But even he looks shocked and unsettled by Ana's feet, his skin taking on a faint green tinge as he looks down at it.

"Fuck, Sofia," he whispers. "I've never seen anything like this. Whoever did this to her—"

"Was it the Bratva?" I ask, my voice trembling as I try to hold back the tears.

"It must have been. I can't think of anyone else who would do something so horrific. The tortures they inflict—makes what I've done look like a spa treatment. I don't want to tell you what else they might have—" he breaks off, his skin waxy as he takes in Ana's appearance. "We need to get her in the bath and warm her up, wash as much blood off as we can."

Luca helps me cut what's left of her clothes off, but there's nothing sexual about it. He does it efficiently and clinically, and when she's finally nude, and we can put her into the warm bath, her bruised body looks so frail and pale that it makes my heart hurt to see it. She's breathing shallowly, and I kneel down next to the tub, my vision blurry with emotion.

"Can you bring me a stack of washcloths?" I ask Luca, and he nods briskly, returning with a handful of them from the linen closet in a matter of seconds. They're all expensive, whatever luxury brand his housekeeper buys with the budget she's given, but he clearly doesn't care.

I look up at him for just one second. At that moment, I get a glimpse of him with his shirt and hands bloodied, his hair a mess, his face flecked with that same blood, and I remember another night in this penthouse when I looked up at him, and he was the same way.

It makes me realize how far we've come, even in just a short time. How different things are. You wouldn't think a week could make that much of a difference, but I can feel how much closer we've grown. We moved like a team, getting Ana inside, and now we do the same, Luca handing me a washcloth and waiting to take the one I have when it gets too dirty and give me a fresh one.

Slowly, keeping an eye on her breathing the entire time, I clean the blood and dirt and vomit off of my best friend. I rinse her hair, running my fingers carefully through the thick blonde locks until they're as clean as I can manage, and then carefully wash her face, using the washcloth and the tip of my finger to clean the blood away from her eyes and nose and bruised lips.

Luca doesn't say a word, just takes the bloody cloths and, at one point, drains and refills the tub when the water gets too pink and dirty as I hold her, watching her breathing the entire time.

I can't stop the tears when I get to her cut and broken feet. "She's a ballerina," I whisper, not able to even look at Luca. "Her whole life, her whole career—it's gone. She won't be able to dance again, not like she used to. There's no way."

"I know." Luca's jaw is tight, his expression hard. "Sofia, I swear, I'll kill whoever did this to her." I can see the muscles working in his cheeks as he looks down at Ana. "If it was the Bratva—it's my fault for sending her in. I'll make this right, I swear."

It could be my fault, too, I think, and I feel sick all over again. I'd asked Ana to do reconnaissance for me, too. It wasn't only Luca who put her in this position, though he doesn't know that. It could be either of us who asked her to do the thing that left her this way.

When she's as clean as she's going to be, her skin warm to the touch and her breathing slightly more regular, Luca helps me dry her off with soft, fluffy towels and wrap her in one of the guest robes. We both carry her to the couch, and while she lies there, Luca brings me a first-aid kit, and I gently put ointment and gauze anywhere that it seems it might help. While I'm patching her up, Luca comes to sit next to me on the floor, something else that I've never seen him do.

"I'm sorry," he says out of the blue, looking over at me.

"What?" I glance at him, startled. "For this? We're not sure if it's the Bratva, but if it was, Luca—she agreed to it, too. I think—"

"No," he interrupts me. "In the bathroom, you said that Ana won't dance again. That her entire career was snatched from her because of this. Her life. And I realized—I did that to you, too."

My hands go very still, the tube of ointment shaking in my fingers. Of all the things I expected to hear from Luca, this is definitely not one of them.

"You had a life before you married me. A potential career as a violinist. A good one, too, I'm told. And I took that away from you. It was to save your life, and I'd do it again—but I never acknowledged that you'd lost something. Only that I felt you were ungrateful about what you'd been given." He smiles at me tightly; his jaw still tense. "I'm not good at apologies, Sofia. I have very little practice with them. But if you'll accept this one, when this is all over—I'll find some way to make it up to you. I promise."

I feel as if all the air has been sucked out of me as if I can't breathe. This is what I've wanted, *all* I wanted for a long time, for Luca to acknowledge that while I, of course, was glad he saved my life, he also took so much from me. All of my plans, all of my future that I'd laid out and worked so hard for.

I'd thought that apology would never come. But here it is.

And I can tell that he means it.

I wonder if it's the right time to tell him about the baby. To ask for a fresh start with him, to make a family, a life together to replace the one I lost when we were married. Once again, it's on the tip of my tongue to confess, to have the conversation that I know I can't put off forever unless I find a way to leave.

Before I can say anything, though, Ana groans behind us, a deep sound of pain that makes us both whirl around to look at her.

"S—Sofia?" Her voice is cracked and hoarse, and my skin crawls hearing it because I remember what it was like to sound just like that. I know that sound now—it's the sound you make when your throat is raw from screaming, and I remember all too vividly how I got to that point in the safe house with Rossi and his men.

"I'm here." I reach for her hand gently. "Luca is too."

Her eyes flick to him nervously. "Luca. I'm—sorry." She tries to swallow, and Luca hands me a glass of water, which I carefully tip at the edge of her lips, helping her lift her head so that she can take a small sip.

"It's alright," he says, moving closer to me. "Whoever did this to you, I'll find them. But I need to know. Was it the Bratva? One of the brigadiers?"

Ana shakes her head. "No," she manages, taking another sip. Her eyes are only half-open, the lids too swollen. She licks her lips and winces, moaning again in pain.

"Who, Ana?" Luca's hands clench into fists. "I know it hurts. But someone needs to answer for this, and I need to know before they strike again. Who did this to you?"

Ana's eyes flick between the two of us, and I see real fear in her face. "I—can't—"

"You have to," Luca insists. "Whoever it is, I'll believe you. But I need you to tell me the truth. I can't help you or anyone if I don't know."

Ana looks at me helplessly.

"Tell him," I urge her, and I see a flicker of surprise in her expression. "Who did it?"

She lets out a slow, shaky breath. "Franco," she whispers.

"What?" Luca and I say it at almost the same time. "Are you sure?" I ask, even as I know how ridiculous that question is. Of course, she's sure. Of course, she knows who it is who hurt her to this degree. But it doesn't make any sense.

"It was Franco," she repeats, her eyes sliding shut. "He—did...this. To...me."

And then she slumps back again, her breathing slow and shallow as she slips back into unconsciousness.

"Fuck," Luca hisses, his eyes trailing over Ana. "I don't fucking believe it."

"She doesn't have any reason to lie."

"No, I know that." He grits his teeth. "I just don't understand why he would—" Luca stands abruptly then, every inch of him tense and angry. "I'm going to go talk to him. I'm going to figure this shit out."

He looks at me. "Stay with her," he says as if I had a choice or would do anything else. And then, to my surprise, he drops a kiss on the top of my head before he strides towards the front door.

My head is spinning as I watch him leave. I can't fathom why Franco would do something like this. I can't think of any reason unless—

I can feel my pulse speeding up, my heart pounding in my chest. If he found out what I asked Ana to do...

Oh god, don't let it be that. Please don't let it be that.

I sit with her until she starts to wake up again, hours later, and this time she's a bit more lucid. "Sofia," she whispers, reaching for my hand, and I lean against the side of the couch, struggling not to cry. "My...feet..."

"I know." I swallow hard, squeezing her hand gently. "I'm so sorry."

"I found out...some things." Ana wheezes slightly, swallowing. "About your mother. She was important, back in Russia—or her father was, at least. He was the second in command to their *Pakhan*. Viktor's equivalent, in Moscow. And she was supposed to make a good marriage, and her husband would have inherited a lot of power. She came from a line of very powerful counts."

"Fuck." I stare at Ana. "And my father basically swept her away and brought her here, into the Italian mafia."

"It was a huge problem," Ana confirms. "It almost started a war. And so when Viktor decided he wanted to move into Rossi's territory, he wanted you. As the daughter of a powerful Italian man and a Russian woman descended from a powerful family, you could have given him more legitimacy as his wife."

"So he didn't want to sell me? He wanted to—"

"Marry you. Yes."

"So now—" I sit back, letting out a slow breath. "He won't want me now."

"Probably not," Ana says quietly. "You're not a virgin, you're married—and not easily divorced, being Catholic—and to make matters worse, you're carrying Luca's child. His *heir*. Going to Viktor isn't going to solve your problem because he would almost certainly make a condition of any kind of help that you terminate the pregnancy. Otherwise, the baby could grow up to decide that he or she wanted revenge and to take their father's territory back. He won't risk that." She looks at me sadly. "I'm sorry, Sofia. I wanted to help. But I don't know what you can do. The Russians aren't a way out."

I nod. "I'm doing this to save my baby. So it doesn't make sense—"

"Sofia, there's something else," Ana says urgently. "Something really important—"

She's cut off by the sound of the front door slamming open. I whirl around, tensed for intruders, my heart pounding in my chest as I choke back the immediate fear.

But it's not the Bratva. It's Luca, back from talking to Franco.

And he looks *furious*.

"Sofia." His voice is deadly calm, and I know then and there that something awful has happened, something to make him angry with me all over again. "Get the fuck upstairs. *Now*."

I start to argue, not wanting to leave Ana. But one look at his face tells me not to.

For the first time in our marriage, I don't fight him.

I just get up and go upstairs.

LUCA

16

"You fucking betrayed me." I can barely contain my rage—and now, on top of that, my hurt.

I'd let my guard down with Sofia. I'd started to trust her. Worse than that, I'd started to *fall* for her.

Only to come back home and find out that she was plotting against me all along.

I knew it. I knew it was a game. I should never have let myself think differently.

"What are you talking about—" Sofia starts to say, and I can feel myself shaking with fury.

"Don't fucking lie to me!" I roar, my voice filling the room. "I'm fucking sick of the lies! You *know* what I'm talking about. You and Ana plotted to double-cross me. I sent her in to find information to save *you*, to help bring peace, and the entire time she was looking for a way to get Viktor to help you escape. You were going to help the fucking Russians in order to get out of here. Why? I don't know, and I don't fucking care. You betrayed me, you bitch, and you and your friend will pay for it."

Sofia is crying now, her face red and streaked with tears, but I don't care. I can't ever remember being so angry, on the verge of coming apart with it. Not when she fought me so many times before, on so many different things, not the other times she'd lied, not when she'd tried to run away.

Because then, at least I hadn't been fucking falling in love with her.

I know, of course, why she was trying to barter with the Russians, why she was trying to run. The baby. She didn't trust me not to force her to follow the letter of the contract. But I don't want her to know that I know that. I want her to tell me herself. Before, because I wanted her to trust me with it. Now, because I want her to just not lie about one fucking thing.

"You wouldn't have gotten far," I sneer at her. "That bracelet you used to wear all the time because I gave it to you, and it was soooo romantic?" I mock her voice, mine rising in pitch. "There was a tracking device in it. That's how I found you in the safe house. And it's not the only piece of jewelry you have that has one. So when you inevitably took some with you to sell, like the greedy little whore you are, I would have been able to follow you."

"You had a tracking device in my *jewelry?*" Sofia looks horrified, and I can't help but laugh.

"Of course I fucking did. You couldn't be trusted, and you proved me right to do it when you ran off. If I hadn't done that, you'd be six feet under right now, tortured to death and raped by Rossi's goons. So don't tell me that you're pissed I put a little chip in your diamond bracelet."

"How do you know about all of this?" she whispers, but I can see from her face that she already knows.

"Franco told me." My voice is full of every bit of the disgust I feel. "You think there's any room in this house that isn't under some kind of surveillance? If not cameras, then microphones. He found evidence of your little setup with Anastasia. He beat her until she admitted to it. And then when I went over there, pissed as fuck because he'd beaten a woman and your best friend half to death, he told me everything."

"Luca, I—"

"Shut the fuck up," I growl. "I was starting to trust you, *wife*. I believed you when you apologized to me for running away. I believed you when you said you wanted the honeymoon so that we could get away together, but it was really just so Anastasia would have more time to execute your little plan, wasn't it? Fuck, I was even starting to have feelings for you." I shake my head, glaring at her. "Rossi was right," I spit out. "I'm weak. You make me weak, but no more."

I don't get close to her the way I usually do when we fight. I don't crowd her space because I don't want to be in it. I don't want that heat to flare between us. I don't want to want her. I want her to stay far the fuck away from me because every problem I've had in my life for the last several months all comes back to her.

And I'm fucking done.

I reach into my pocket, fishing out the necklace that I'd taken off of Rossi's body. Her mother's necklace. "I was going to give this back to you on the honeymoon," I growl, clenching it in my fist. "I didn't get a chance to. I was too *distracted.* But you can fucking have it back now." I throw it at her, watching it fall to the floor at her feet, and when Sofia scoops it up off of the floor, fresh tears start streaming down her face.

It makes me sick to see it. This act. She was a devious little traitor all along.

"My mother's necklace—Rossi took this."

"And I took it back from him. I should have thrown it in the fucking ocean." I glare at her. "I should kill Ana for what she did. I should kill *you*, but if not you, then her for certain. Someone has to pay for this treachery."

"No!" Sofia almost screams it, her eyes going wide with terror. "Please, Luca, no." She steps towards me, and I take a step back, not wanting her close to me.

"I'll beg," she whispers. "I'll get on my knees. I'll do anything you want. She's paid enough. All that torture, that hurt, the beatings, her whole career gone—Luca, she's paid. Please don't kill her. You can do anything to me. But please, please—"

"I want nothing from you but your obedience," I growl, my jaw clenching. "Anastasia will live, for now. But you will not leave this apartment. You will not step a foot out of place. I'm leaving today for the conclave, and when I come back, I'll decide what to do about you both. Until then, I'm leaving Franco here to guard you and make certain that you don't leave."

Sofia gasps. "Franco? Are you serious? After what he did—"

I smile cruelly at her. "That's exactly why I'm leaving him," I tell her flatly. "If need be, I know he'll do what needs to be done." I pause, holding her gaze. "If I'd gone to him and found out that he'd brutalized Ana for no reason, as I thought, then he'd be dead now. But instead, I found that he was just punishing a traitor. And that is him doing exactly as I've told him he needed to."

Sofia is staring at me in horror, her mouth hanging open.

"You'd be wise to watch your behavior very carefully," I tell her. "You're on thin ice now. You and Anastasia both."

And with that, I turn on my heel and leave.

Once I'm in my office, I can breathe a little. I feel sick, betrayed, angrier than I've ever been. *This is why I didn't want to fall for her,* I think furiously, leaning forward and gripping the edge of my desk. I never thought I could be taken in by someone like her, but after all this time, little virgin Sofia Ferretti was the one to do it.

I'd wanted her more than any other woman.

I'd been falling in love with her.

For fuck's sake, I'd almost *said* it on the goddamn honeymoon. But I wanted to wait for her to tell me about the baby, to come clean with me, and ask for a new start. I'd hoped she might tell me when I'd apologized to her for ruining her career.

What a laughable fucking thing to do. I feel like a fool now for ever saying that. And she was never going to tell me about the baby. She might not even want it. She just wants to escape. Even if that means selling secrets to my enemy and setting me up to lose everything I've worked so hard for.

I sold my soul for the mafia. I'm not going to lose out on the deal.

Keeping her in line isn't the only reason I'm leaving Franco here. Especially after this debacle, I'm not entirely sure the conclave will go well. Deep down, I have a bad gut feeling about it. And if something were to happen to me, I want Franco to still be alive so that there's someone I know I can trust to take over.

If I'm dead, he'll probably execute Anastasia and Sofia both. But I'm past putting everything on the line for my lovely, traitorous wife.

She's going to have to fall in line and tell me everything, or I'm done with her. Done with the promises, done with trying to be a husband to a woman who can't be a wife.

It's time for me to be the ruthless man I was raised to be.

SOFIA

17

I wait until I'm sure Luca is gone to emerge from the bedroom. The first thing I do is go and get Ana, who is half-awake again. I get her up the stairs somehow, very slowly, all the way to my old room, where I plan to stay with her until Luca comes back. There's no way I'm leaving her alone for even a second, especially if Franco is going to be watching us.

I lay next to her on the bed for a long time as she sleeps. She'll need to eat something when she wakes up, and I wish for the thousandth time that we'd taken her to a hospital. When she'd said it was Franco, I'd had some hope that we could do exactly that, now that we knew the Bratva wasn't lying in wait. But Luca's discovery ruined that small hope.

Does he know about the baby? If he'd heard the conversation in the bathroom, then he must—unless Franco didn't show him the whole conversation.

Unless he kept that bit of information back to use as leverage later.

During our argument, I couldn't read Luca's face well enough to figure out if he knew. He was angrier than I've ever seen him, and I've seen him in rages that have terrified me. There was no electric charge between us this time, no heat turning the furious argument into something filthy and sexual.

This time he was cold. He wanted nothing to do with me.

And that's somehow even more terrifying.

If Luca doesn't know about the baby, then that buys me a little time, at least. If he does, then likely he'll come back from the conclave with his decisions—and one of those will be a trip to the hospital for me to put an unwilling end to it.

I have no plan anymore. No way for me to get out. No way to escape.

I'm hemmed in. And even if I could figure out some plan, there's no way Ana could go with me. And I can't leave her here like this. If I run away and leave her behind, I know either Franco or Luca will kill her.

It's very late before she wakes up again. I made some soup, and I set it on a tray in front of her, intending to help her eat it.

"You're a good friend," Ana says weakly as I help her with the first bite. "The best." She swallows, trying to breathe evenly through her bruised and possibly broken nose. "Is Luca still here?"

I shake my head. "He left for the conclave. He talked to Franco—" I take a deep breath, and I can see the fear in her face just at the mention of his name. "Franco told him about our plan. That he'd found out, and that's why he did this to you."

Ana nods. "That's why I didn't want to admit it. I'd hoped I could pin it on the Bratva—but Luca would have found out I was lying. And it would have started a war. I wasn't sure which was worse."

"You did fine," I promise her. "Luca was furious. Things were getting better between us, but they definitely aren't now. I don't think they ever will be again. He feels like I've betrayed him, and in a way, he's right."

"Does he know about the baby?"

"I don't know," I admit. "But I haven't told him. If he knows, then he found out some other way."

Ana winces. "I'm so sorry, Sofia. I tried—"

"Shhh." I soothe her, helping her with another bite of soup. "I know you did. It's not your fault. It's mine that this happened to you. I should never have asked you to do that. I should have known there'd be something in this fucking place that could hear us, that would get us both in trouble—"

"You were desperate," Ana says softly. "I can't say that I wouldn't have done the same. I'm not angry with you, Sofia. You were in an impossible position."

"Really?" I bite my lower lip, trying not to cry. "You really feel that way?"

"I do," she promises, swallowing another bite of soup. "But there's something else I need to tell you, Sofia. Something I found out after going to bed with one of the brigadiers, Leo."

"What?" I set down the spoon, my heart skipping a beat in my chest.

"Luca might feel you're a traitor, but you're not the real traitor in his ranks," she says softly, so softly that no one outside the door lurking could possibly hear. "Sofia—it's Franco."

For a moment, I just stare at her dumbly, much the way I did when she said his name earlier this afternoon.

"He didn't just beat me almost to death because of our conversation. It was because he knew I was on the verge of, or had already found out, information about what *he* was doing. And my god, Sofia, it's bad."

"What did you find out?" My mind is reeling. If there's a way to take Franco down, to prove he was lying to Luca all along, then anything he said about me is discredited. Luca might have heard a tape, but that doesn't mean I can't try to spin it somehow if Franco's integrity is thrown enough into question.

At least enough to save Ana's life and mine.

"You know all the rumors about Franco's parentage?" Ana asks, and I nod. Luca's mentioned it before. "Well," she continues, her voice cracking a little from the strain. "They're true."

"They're...what?"

"His father is Irish," Ana confirms. "And not just Irish, but *the* Irish. Colin Macgregor, the king of the Irish mob. He and Franco's mother had an affair, just as the rumors go. Of course, Rossi made her take a paternity test, and she faked it. Bribed the administrator to change the results. So the test result that Rossi had in that safe in Luca's office is false. Franco is Colin's son."

"But—how does that affect the Bratva?"

"Viktor has the real results, the ones that tell Franco's real parentage," Ana says, her voice a hushed whisper. "And he's hanging it over Franco's head to get him to betray Luca. Franco has been feeding the Russians secrets all this time, helping them gain ground."

"So he's at least partially responsible for Caterina's mother's death." I frown. "I don't know if Luca will care about the parentage all that much, Ana. He's not as traditional as Rossi was. He might not care if Franco is half-Irish. He'll almost certainly see that as Colin Macgregor's betrayal and Franco's mother. He won't see it as Franco's fault. And as much as I want Franco gone after what he did to you, I can't say that he'd be wrong about that. It's not Franco's fault his mother cheated, and the fact that Rossi would have killed him for it, that it's even something to hang over Franco's head, is awful. Franco is his best friend—Luca has been protecting him all his life. It's going to be hard for anything to break that."

"The affair isn't his fault, sure. But Luca will care about the betrayal, though," Ana points out, and I know she's right. "And he'll care about the rest of it, too."

"There's more?" I lean back against the pillows, staring at her. *How far is this going to go?* Less than forty-eight hours ago, I would never have dreamed that any of this would have happened—that Ana would be so brutally injured, much less that Franco, Luca's best friend, would be responsible for it. And not just that—but the betrayal that's been haunting us all.

"Franco and Colin Macgregor—his father—are working together." Ana's face looks very pale as she explains it to me—all of the pieces she managed to uncover. I feel a chill run over my arms as I listen.

"I wonder if Caterina knows about any of this," I whisper. "I can't imagine she would go along with it—"

"I don't think she does." Ana frowns. "I don't think Franco would trust her with it and is Caterina really that loyal to Franco? Don't you think she would tell Luca if her husband was plotting something like this?"

"Probably. She grew up with Luca. Her father and his were best friends. Her father was Luca's mentor. Franco rose to the position he's in because of the trust Rossi and Luca had in him. Caterina isn't in love with him. She's loyal to him because he's her husband, but if it came down to it and she knew he had a part in something like that, she'd tell Luca."

"What are *you* going to do about Luca?" Ana shifted uncomfortably, and I reached for the tray, sliding it further down the bed now that she was done with her soup. "You said before this, things were getting better?"

I nod, reaching for a bottle of painkillers, shaking a few out into my palm, and handing them to her. "I did what you said. I made him think I was sorry for running away, apologized to him, seduced him."

"Not exactly the worst thing in the world," Ana said with a small laugh. "He might be an asshole a lot of the time, Sofia, but your husband is fucking hot." She winces, shifting a little. "The mission to infiltrate the Bratva wasn't so bad either. A couple of the brigadiers were gorgeous. And not bad in bed, either, for men that are supposed to be selfish asses. I should have gotten some Russian gangster dick a long time ago, honestly."

"Oh my god, Ana!" I try not to laugh, but a moment later, we're both dissolving into giggles. Ana gasps, trying to catch her breath.

"It hurts to laugh." She presses one hand to her stomach, leaning her head back. "Oh god, Sofia, did you ever think we'd be here? You married to the head of the mafia, me fucking Bratva soldiers for information, both of us wrapped up in all of this intrigue, getting kidnapped and tortured and—Christ, this is fucked up."

"It really is." I bite my lip, looking at her. "God, I'm sorry, Ana. I never wanted anything like this to happen to you."

"That makes two of us." She leans back on the pillows, trying to take a deep breath. "So tell me the rest of what happened with Luca. Take my mind off of this until the ibuprofen kicks in. Not to mention

—Sofia, your husband is a fucking high-end drug dealer, arms runner, and all-around white-collar criminal. Can't you find a fucking Vicodin somewhere?"

I choke back another laugh. "I'll see what I can do." It feels good to laugh, despite the situation. "Maybe I can convince someone from the security team to dig some up for you."

"I don't know how well that's going to work, with Franco in charge." Ana winces just at the mention of his name. "I can't believe we're stuck here with him. After what he did to me—" she shudders, and I see tears forming at the corners of her eyes. I can't remember the last time I saw Ana cry, but she looks like she's on the verge of it now. It makes me helplessly, furiously angry.

"I never thought Luca would do something like that," Ana whispers, rubbing at her eyes. "Fuck. I don't want to start crying."

"You've been through something awful. Maybe you need a good cry."

"Maybe later. In the bath, where no one can hear me." Ana's mouth crooks up a little. "Although I guess in this place, there's no telling where someone can hear me."

"A couple of days ago, I wouldn't have thought Luca would do something like this either. Things were so different on our honeymoon."

"That's where you went? You got him to take you on a *honeymoon?*" Ana looks at me in disbelief, and I laugh.

"Yeah. I didn't think it would work either. I wanted to give you some time without Luca on you about what you were finding out from the Bratva. But I guess that backfired too."

"It's not your fault," Ana reassures me. "You couldn't possibly have guessed Franco would do that or that he'd find out by some microphone hidden in the one room we thought was safe. We tried our best." She reaches for my hand, squeezing it lightly. "Things just got fucked up, that's all. We couldn't have known."

"That whole week was so different. We had that little period of time where things were good, but this was a totally new level. I was—"

"Falling for him?" Ana supplies. "I had a feeling it might happen if Luca ever stopped being a grade-A ass for more than five minutes."

"Really?"

She shrugs. "Sofia, I know you're hung up on him being in the mafia, and the fact that you didn't choose to marry him, and his overall attitude towards you—and basically all women, if we're being honest. But he's got a lot of admirable qualities, too."

I narrow my eyes at her. "That's weird, considering he's currently thinking about having us both killed."

Ana sighs. "Sofia, your father tried hard to shelter and protect you. But sometimes, I think he did too good of a job. This is a different world from the one you're used to. A different life." She pauses, considering. "Do you think Caterina is weak?"

"What?" I look at her, surprised. "Of course not. She's one of the toughest women I know. She's been through so much recently, but she's still pushing forward, doing her best to—"

"That's my point," Ana interrupts. "Caterina was raised in this life, aware of what was going on, of the way the men are. Aware of the things they have to do, the walls they have to put up in order to deal with that. Some of them take pleasure in it, I'm sure, but men like Luca don't. He's threatening us because he feels he has to because he feels betrayed and can't allow that. It would make him look weak. And—"

"And what?" I can't quite believe what she's saying, especially in her state. "How can you say that, after what he did—"

"Franco did this, not Luca. I don't know Luca well, but I'm certain he would never do anything like this to a woman. Possibly not anyone. There's torture—and then there's what Franco did." She swallows hard. "Sofia, Luca *asked* me to infiltrate the Bratva."

"I know he did, but—"

"No, you're not hearing me. He *asked*." Ana looks pointedly at me. "He could have ordered me. He could have threatened me. Franco tried to talk him out of it—probably because he was afraid I'd find out exactly what I did. But Luca *asked* me to do it. He appealed to my friendship with you. He talked me into it. He didn't use demands or threats. That's someone who only uses violence when necessary. And not just that."

"What do you mean?"

"I think he was falling for you, too. He's angry not just because he feels betrayed but because it was *you*. What was he like on the honeymoon?"

"Perfect." The word surprises me even as I say it, but it's the first one that comes to mind. "He flew us to Mustique and bought out the whole island, so it was only us. He even remembered the exact brand of champagne we had at our wedding and brought it on the flight. Everything was different, even the sex. He was sweet and romantic and—" the last word is hard to say, but I manage it anyway. "Loving."

My chest aches all over again, and I feel my eyes burning. "I felt like I could fall in love with him. Like we were falling in love with each other. And I was so happy, and so sad all at once because it felt so good, but it didn't change anything. I knew I still needed to leave because of the baby. And then when we came back, and we found you —we worked as a team. For the first time, it was like we were real partners. He helped me bring you inside and get you into the bath. He brought me everything I needed to clean you up. I couldn't have asked for someone better to be there with me to help keep me calm. And then afterward, while we were waiting for you to wake up—" I take an unsteady breath, my heart hurting all over again at the memory. "He apologized to me for what I lost when we got married. My education, my career as a violinist. He *really* apologized."

"Seriously?"

"He said he realized it when he saw your feet and realized what was taken from you. He said he realized what he'd taken from me. And he was sorry."

"Shit." Ana whistled softly. "It really was getting better then. And then he found out what we did."

"I almost told him about the baby when he apologized. I guess it's good that I didn't." I pause, remembering our conversation over dinner. "I asked him about how he would feel about being a father while we were on our honeymoon. And he answered me seriously.

The answer wasn't what I expected either—he said he'd want a son to continue his legacy but that he wouldn't force a daughter into the same position Caterina or I were in. It sounded—it almost sounded as if he *wanted* kids. And I had some hope—"

"Don't give up hope yet." Ana squeezes my hand. "Luca doesn't know yet about what Franco's done. Our betrayal might seem a little less serious in the wake of that. You forgave him once, he might still be inclined to forgive you."

"What about the baby?"

"Worry about that when he comes back. You have some time still before you start showing. There's no reasonable way out right now anyway. So when Luca returns, talk to him. Try to reason with him. He might just need some time to calm down."

It strikes me suddenly that Luca is headed to the conclave, with no idea about Franco's betrayal.

"Shit, Ana. Someone needs to tell Luca. Someone has to warn him about Franco—"

"Viktor is going to talk to him at the conclave," she says tiredly. "He found out what Franco did with Colin. He's going to tell Luca everything, and they'll confront the Irish. That's the other reason the Bratva isn't a way out for you. He's going to align himself with the mafia again, so he's not going to risk that by getting you out."

"What's going to happen to Franco?"

"Hopefully, they'll fucking kill him." There's a bitter note in Ana's voice, and I can hardly blame her. If I'd had the chance to kill Rossi with my own bare hands, I would have relished it. And Franco did that and worse to her.

"Can you help me to the bath?" She turns to look at me, and I can see that she's gone pale again. "I think a hot bath might do me some good."

SOFIA

18

*O*nce I help Ana into the huge jacuzzi bath, I wander through the penthouse, too anxious and fidgety to sit still. The one room that I've never been in is Luca's study. I find myself wandering that way, even though I know there are probably security cameras in there or some shit that's going to get me in terrible trouble if I manage to get in.

It's probably locked anyway. Luca would never leave his study open; it's the one room he's super careful about.

But when I try the knob, to my surprise, it turns. He must have been so angry when he left that he overlooked locking it.

Shit. I pause, my hand on the doorknob, my heart racing. *Do I risk it? Do I go in?*

What the hell. I'm already in the most trouble I can be in, right? Surely after what Luca and I argued about, my sneaking into his office is the least of my worries. I slip inside, closing the door behind me.

I've been in here once before, just after Luca told me that we were going to be married. But I hadn't looked around much then. I'd been too terrified, just trying to stand my ground enough to have some kind of bargaining power in what was about to happen to my life.

Now I actually take in the room. It's not really anything special—

luxurious and elegant, like the rest of the penthouse, but a fairly standard office. If anything, it reminds me of my father's office in my childhood home, with the usual giant mahogany desk, leather chairs for guests, and floor-to-ceiling bookshelves. There are the traditional classics on the shelves, but as I walk past them, running my fingers over the spines, I realize that there's more than just books for show here. There are more books like the one Luca was reading on the plane—novels he must actually like reading. Science-fiction mysteries, space operas, techno-thrillers set in the future. There's a lot of Philip K. Dick mixed in, and I touch each book, thinking about Luca sitting in here at his desk, reading. Maybe with his feet up on the mahogany, a tumbler of whisky in his hand.

It's such a normal, human image that it startles me. For a long time, I saw my husband as this terrifying monster, a man to be afraid of, to watch out for. A man who did terrible things, who lived in a world saturated in violence and blood. A man who inspired fear and awe in others rather than love.

But looking at this reminds me of the Luca that I shared a week with on a private island. The man that I was falling in love with.

And Ana seems to think that there's something there still to salvage. Something to love, if I can convince him to keep our baby. That we could build a family together worth having.

I want to believe that. I realize, stroking the spine of a science-fiction novel and thinking about a life without Luca, alone and on the run, that I want it as much as I once wanted my months in Paris and my seat in the London orchestra.

But it would mean that I would have to be stronger than I am now. I would have to step up and be a wife that Luca could depend on. A wife like Caterina. Someone who can take the violence and the strife of the mafia in stride.

I would have to be okay with my child—*our* child—being at Luca's side if it was a boy—or maybe even a girl. I remember him clearly saying that the ways of the mafia can change, that he might let a daughter inherit.

I would have to be not only devoted to Luca, but to the mafia itself.

A marriage to a don, a *real* marriage, means marrying the family as well, in a much greater sense than the old saying goes. I would have to not flinch at the things my child—or children, would grow up to do.

If I stay, I can't resent the mafia and the things that Luca does as the head of it. I have to accept it.

I don't know if I'm that strong. But I want to be.

I think of my father's letter and how much he wanted me to escape all of this. But surely, since he left this failsafe for me, he thought I was strong enough to withstand a marriage to a man like Luca, to be the wife of a man with real power in this family.

All fairytales have a dark side.

The book of fairytales that my father left me wasn't a book of frilly children's stories about balls and princesses who lived happily ever after. In those Grimm's fairytales, the princesses and heroines had to work for their happy endings. They had to make sacrifices. Sometimes they exacted terrible revenge, like Cinderella, who made her stepsisters dance in red-hot shoes.

Those women knew their lives weren't pretty, or sweet, or easy. That they'd have nothing unless they fought for it. They knew what it meant to love the darkness.

I used to think he gave me that book just because he thought I'd like it, but now I think it was because he knew what my life might become. That I might have to learn how to be Persephone wedded to Hades, instead of a cartoon Cinderella with mice for servants and a bland prince for a husband.

That I, the daughter of an Italian mafia consigliere and a Russian heiress, would be used as a bargaining chip in a game that I have no desire to play. A chess piece on a board that I desperately wanted to get off of.

But now, I think that maybe I want to take my spot next to the king.

I think about Luca and our honeymoon. I think about the moments we've shared. I think about our child growing in my belly, and then I think about the man guarding me right now. This man calls himself Luca's best friend, the man who married above his station, the man who tortured *my* best friend and cost her everything.

I think about it, and I feel like Cinderella, making her sisters dance on hot glass.

I want revenge. I don't want to run and hide and cower. I want Luca to listen to me, believe me, and give me a place at his side. I'm angry not just for myself, not just for Ana, but for Luca too, I realize. Luca gave Franco *everything*. His friendship and loyalty and trust, protection from his bullies, a bulwark against the rumors and lies that turned out to be true after all. He gave him a beautiful mafia princess for his wife, a place at his right hand. And what did Franco Bianchi do with all of that?

He lied and betrayed his best friend. He plotted against him, not just with one rival mob but two. He treated his wife as less than the treasured gift that she was. And now he's all but destroyed the one person in the world that I love besides my husband.

Because I do love Luca. It's a love that's grown out of hate, but standing here in this moment, I know that the feelings I had for him on the island were real.

He's my husband, for better or for worse. And I want to be a real wife to him.

I look at the bookshelf again, my hand sliding over the spines, and I see a small leather volume tucked in with the rest. It's thin, the spine slightly cracked, and when I pull it out, I realize it's not a book at all.

It's a journal.

Luca keeps a journal? It seems so strange for him, so out of character. I could imagine Luca sitting at his desk in the evenings and reading, but writing out his feelings in a journal? It's so far beyond the image of him that I have in my head that I want to laugh.

But I don't laugh. I sit down at the desk, knowing that I'm intruding on Luca's privacy. *He's invaded my privacy plenty of times,* I think wryly as I open the cover. After everything he's done to me, I shouldn't really feel weird about reading his private journal. But I do feel a little bit like I'm doing something that I shouldn't.

Still, I can't resist my curiosity and the possibility of being able to humanize my husband a little bit more, to understand him.

It's not written in flowery prose, but I wouldn't have expected it to be. What it is, is more of a stream of consciousness, Luca's thoughts as if he just couldn't keep them in any longer. It's like blood being spilled out onto a page, and once I start reading, I can't stop.

I don't know what's happened to me. I can't stop fucking thinking about her. Those lips, that ass, I want to fucking ruin her. She wants me to leave her a virgin, and I don't know how I can do that. It's like she's fucking torturing me.

It goes on like that for a while. *I thought taking her virginity would make me stop needing her. But I just want her more. She's like fucking cocaine, but better. Like pure ecstasy. Raw, uncut, untouched until I made her mine.*

But then, around the time that he took me on that rooftop date, something changed. The entries get a little softer, a little sweeter. *I had no idea she liked action movies too. I also had no idea I'd like watching a movie with my wife.*

Spoiling Sofia is better than I could have ever imagined. The look on her face every time she sees some new beautiful thing or tries something she's never had to eat or drink before is more endearing than I would have ever thought.

I almost lost her. But if anyone touches her, I'll slaughter the entire Bratva. I'll kill every fucking Russian in the country if I have to.

I keep skimming through it, my heart speeding up as I read passage after passage. They're not long entries, as if Luca just quickly scribbled these down when he couldn't keep it in any longer.

And then I see the entry just after he saved me from Rossi.

I don't know how to feel. I'm furious at her for leaving. I want to strangle her, and at the same time, I want to hold her close, keep her next to me so that nothing like this can ever happen to her again. I'm both infuriated by her stubborn refusal to let me protect her and amazed at her strength. I've seen men break after less than what Rossi and his men did to her. But she's still alive. She's still fighting. And as angry as I am, I can't change how I feel. But I need to make sure that no one can use her against me ever again. That no one will take her and hurt her to get to me. And that means making sure that she can't possibly love me. That I can't love her. That there's nothing to destroy or hurt.

But that means I have to hurt her heart. I have to break her and make sure she fears me. I don't know of any other way to stop this from growing into something more.

And then later on, just before our honeymoon.

This is a bad idea. But I can't tell her no.

She's more than an addiction. More than an obsession.

She's the woman I love. And I don't know what to do with that.

I want to love her. But I don't want to be weak, either.

There's nothing more after that. But as I close the journal, clutching it in my hands, I feel tears filling my eyes and spilling down my cheeks. My husband loves me. It doesn't make it okay—but everything he did was to purposefully try to keep me at arm's length so that no one would think they could use me to get to him.

To prevent the exact thing that happened with Rossi.

No wonder he was so angry at me for running away, when he'd gone to such lengths to prevent exactly that.

I press the journal against my chest. When Luca comes home, I'm going to do exactly what Ana suggested. I'm going to reason with him. I'm going to tell him the truth and see if we can find a way to save our marriage. If we can fix what we've broken and move forward together.

Because now I know that my husband loves me. And the truth that I've been running for so long is plain to me now.

I love him too.

LUCA

19

Conclave sounds a lot more arcane and exciting than what the meeting actually is.

In reality, it's less of a secret society meeting and more of a hotel conference room with three arrogant, powerful men, their seconds-in-command—except for me, since I left Franco back in Manhattan—and enough security to create a small army.

The conclave itself is happening in Boston, which is considered as neutral as it gets, despite our close relationship with the Irish. The idea is that the primary conflict is between the Bratva and the Italian mafia. Hence, Manhattan is the site of the impending war. We've moved it out of that hotly contested area and to somewhere a little more neutral. But the energy in the room is anything but neutral.

"I hope you've come to your senses, lad," Colin says flatly as he takes his seat. Next to him is his oldest son Liam Macgregor, the prince of the Irish mob and heir to its leadership. He's a good-looking young man, with hair that's more coppery than flaming red and the build of an MMA fighter. Most of the Irish like to fight, so I wouldn't be surprised if he does plenty of that in his spare time.

The Russians use guns, the Irish use their fists, and we Italians like to use our words. That's what I grew up hearing, anyway. But the truth is that I'm reaching the end of my diplomacy.

"We're here so that we can all come to our senses," I reply as pleasantly as I can. "I hope we can all see reason here today."

"If by 'see reason,' you mean accept that the Russians are responsible for the attack on the hotel, and the deaths that followed, then aye, lad. I'll accept that."

I expect a retort from Viktor, but he looks nonplussed. He sits rigidly in his chair, visibly the oldest of us with the slight silver at his temples and the lines at the corners of his eyes. Still, there's a cold elegance about him that's intimidating, even though I'd never admit it aloud.

"There's plenty that you Irish are responsible for," he says coolly. "And Luca is about to hear all of it." He turns towards me, his expression calm, his blue eyes ice cold. "You're not going to like what I have to say, Romano. But it's the truth. And I'd like to lead by saying that you'll have your peace. I'm agreeable to it."

My face remains expressionless, but inside I can feel that growing sense of foreboding.

"I'm not sure what you're about to say, but I'm pretty sure it's going to be a crock of shite," Colin says, leaning back in his seat.

Viktor smiles coldly, and next to him, Levin grunts as he hands Viktor a file.

I look at Colin. To most, he would look perfectly calm, but I can see something different in his expression, a slight twitch of his eye, like a poker tell.

I'd been prepared not to believe anything Viktor said. But now I'm not so sure.

"I see you didn't bring your underboss," Viktor says as he lays the file on the table. "Why is that, I wonder?"

"After recent incidents, I wanted a trusted pair of eyes on my wife at all times." I smile coolly. "You wouldn't leave a prized piece of art in a museum overnight without security, would you?"

Viktor smirks. "Your wife is indeed as beautiful as any piece of art. More so than some, I'd say. So I can understand the urge. Perhaps I should have left someone at home with my Katerina, and she'd still be alive today."

I don't say anything. I know that story well—but it's from a conflict years ago. "Katerina was an accident," I say calmly. "And I had nothing to do with it."

"Oh, I'm well aware." Viktor rests his hand on the file. "Your underboss, Franco Bianchi, has betrayed you, Luca."

My immediate reaction, as he expected, is disbelief. But underneath that is a tiny flicker of uncertainty. The incident with Ana left me unsettled. He claimed he was just punishing a traitor, making sure that she'd confessed everything she and Sofia had planned. But what he did to her was brutal beyond what was necessary. It was beyond anything I've ever done.

It was beyond even what Rossi and his men had done to Sofia, and that made me sick. It made me question how well I know my best friend—because Franco has never been a brutal man. If anything, I've worried that he didn't have the stomach for the things he might have to do.

But that didn't seem to be the case.

His treatment of Ana had concerned me, but her and Sofia's plotting had infuriated me enough to make me overlook it. But now, as Viktor taps his fingers on the file, my sense of foreboding turns to a feeling of dread.

"I'm not sure I believe you." The words come out of my mouth, but I think Viktor can hear the uncertainty in them.

"That's fine." He smiles. "I have proof. First, you see, your friend betrayed you to us. He was passing along the information to me—he has been for months now, long before you got ahold of your pretty wife. It was him who managed to help set up Sofia's kidnapping in the first place so that I could attempt to be the one who married her."

"That's bullshit." I force my voice to stay even. "He would have had no reason to do that."

"Oh, but he did. You see, the test results for his paternity that Vitto Rossi had are forged. His mother managed to convince someone to do that for her, probably with the same wiles that she used to get Colin Macgregor between her legs."

"Ye're on dangerous ice there, Andreyev," Colin growled, but Viktor ignored him.

"I have the test results here. There are other copies available, from more official places, if you don't believe me. Colin Macgregor is Franco Bianchi's father. Now I'll admit, his working for us happened because I had those test results, and I used them to blackmail him into providing us with information."

"You fucking bastard." I half rise out of my seat, feeling my gut twist with anger. "I don't give a fuck if Franco is half-Irish, half-Polish, or half fucking Greek, so long as he's not half-Russian. His whore mother opening her legs to the Macgregors doesn't concern me."

"Easy there, lad," Colin says, but I ignore him.

"I thought you'd say that." Viktor smiles at me coolly. "But there's more. You see, you believed Franco was loyal to you. And I believed he was betraying you and working for me. But we were both very fucking wrong."

At that moment, I glance sideways at Colin when I see him shift in the corner of my vision. And the expression on his face tells me all I need to know.

Whatever Viktor is about to say, it's not good for the Irish.

And Viktor is telling the truth.

"Franco and Colin, his father, had big plans," Viktor continues with a cold smile. "They intended to pit you and me against each other, and when the dust settled, they'd clear us both out and take over all of the Northeast territories, yours and mine. I was telling the truth when I said it wasn't my men who attacked the wedding. It was the Irish. Colin did that, under Franco's direction, to make you think it was us."

My jaw is clenched so hard I think my teeth might crack. The betrayal is astounding—if it's true. "Do you have proof?" I ask tightly, and that's when Viktor slides the file across the table towards me.

"It's all in there," he says. "The test results. Photos that my men took in secret of Franco and Colin's meeting. Some phone logs I managed to get ahold of. Enough proof for you—"

I don't get to open the file because Colin proves it for me at that moment.

He must have known I was about to see the truth. Because he leaps up, his gun drawn and aimed at me. Next to him, a look of pure horror is written across his son's face.

"Da? What in the bloody hell are you doing?" Liam pushes his chair back.

"Sit down, son!" Colin orders, and I see Liam freeze, but his eyes are darting nervously around. It's clear that whatever Colin has done, Liam was never in on it. And I'll remember that.

"All but the security teams are supposed to give up our weapons before we enter the conclave," I say, as calmly as if Colin weren't pointing a loaded gun right at my head. "This doesn't give me much faith that Viktor is lying."

"Well, I'm tired of playing by the bloody rules," Colin says with a cold grin. "What has that gotten me, eh? Not a single Irish king in Manhattan now, only you bloody lot of Italians and the Russian dogs. We run your guns, pick up your scraps, and we're supposed to bow and thank you for it? Well, no fucking more, lad. What Viktor here said was true. And since it's been made a right mess, I suppose I'll have to finish you both now before this can get any more out of hand."

"You are not the only one who can break the rules." Levin's deep voice booms in the small room, and I see the movement of him sliding a gun out of his jacket.

Fuck! Am I the only one who actually came unarmed? My security is just outside the door, but—

The first shot makes me flinch. A rattle of gunfire comes from outside the room, and I know then with a sinking heart that my security has their hands full, and probably Viktor's, too. And Colin's gun is still trained on my head.

"What do you want for this peace that you're talking about?" I look at Viktor, keeping my voice steady. It's not the first time that a gun's been held to my head, after all.

And I'm sure it won't be the last.

"Colin's head on a platter." Viktor smiles coldly. "I want him dead. Let his son take over. Liam had no part in this, so far as I know."

Colin glances over at his son. "You hear this? They're giving you my place at the table. Are you going to take their offer? Or stand with your da against these fuckers who think we're nothing but whiskey-drinking trash, good only for running their guns and serving at their bars?"

"Da, just think about this," Liam pleads. He stands up, his face so pale his freckles stand out in three dimensions, but he keeps his cool. "You can't go up against both families. Even if you take Victor and Luca both out, they'll be avenged. You'll have the wrath of the mafia and Bratva both on all our heads. Is that what you want? Our women and children enslaved by the Russians, killed by the Italians, our entire family line wiped out? You can't start a war all on your own. No one will stand with you."

"Not even you?" Colin glares at his son. "Like fuck I can't."

Liam licks his lips nervously. He takes a deep breath, looking at his father, and then with a deep sigh, he steps back. "No, Da. I'm sorry. I can't stand with you on this. You're not right. *This* isn't right. This double-dealing and betrayal, it's crossing lines that aren't meant to be crossed." He looks over at us. "I stand with you both. I don't want more bloodshed either."

"See? Your son has some sense." I smile coolly at Colin. "Put the gun down, and we'll give you a quick, clean death. Your son can take over with no hard feelings."

Colin laughs a deep and bitter sound. "Fuck that," he says, his voice loud and clear.

And then he fires.

In the same moment, Liam throws himself at his father. He knocks his arm aside, enough to send the shot wild, but Colin fires twice. I have just enough time to register that the first shot didn't hit me when the second plows into my midsection, sending me to my knees in front of the table.

I swear I can feel the heat where the bullet entered me, the tearing of flesh as it punches a hole in my gut. I automatically clap my hand over my stomach, pitching forward as I feel wet, hot blood spurting over my fingers.

The hotel carpet scrapes against the side of my face as I fall, my head smacking against the floor. The pain spreads through my body, followed by a cold sensation at the edges that I recognize as shock. I'm bleeding out. I can feel my life pumping out over my fingers, soaking my shirt, the carpet, spreading out around me as I hear the continued rattle of gunfire, the shouting, and I know that the fighting is still going on.

But I probably won't be alive to find out how it all ends.

Sofia's face swims in front of my eyes, tearful and pleading, the way I saw her last. I want to remember her the way she was on our honeymoon, her face soft and sweet, her mouth and body yielding underneath mine, her hands sliding over me. I want to remember her voice sweetly whispering to me, not begging, full of desperation.

She betrayed me. Franco betrayed me.

I should hate her. But deep down, I can't. All I can think is that the last thing I ever said to my wife was that I should have her killed.

I love her, and I never said it.

I've spent my whole life living without regrets. But now I know I have one.

Sofia Ferretti is my biggest regret.

Not marrying her. Not loving her. Not putting a baby in her belly.

But never telling her how I felt. Never saying those words. Never letting her know that I wanted our child, too.

And now it's too late.

The sounds of the room fade away as my thoughts stutter and slow, and I feel myself slipping away.

Sofia.
I love you.
I love—
I—

SOFIA

20

I'm still holding on to the journal as I get ready to leave the office. I know I should put it back on the shelf, but I can't bring myself to just yet. I want to read it again, to memorize the words Luca wanted to say to me but didn't. To see him say that he loves me, even if he's never said it.

Even if he never will.

I walk towards the door, still lost in thought. So much so that I don't realize at first that the door is already opening before I can even reach for the knob.

And then it swings open, and Franco is standing there.

There's a gun in his hand.

And it's pointed at me.

"Franco." My voice cracks, and I clear my throat. "I'm just going to bed—"

"What's that?" He nods at the book in my hand. "You stealing now too? Along with betraying your husband?"

"What? No. It's just a book. I wanted to read before I went to sleep—"

"You're not going anywhere." He waves the gun. "Back up. Into the office."

I take an unsteady step backward, my mind racing. *Is this Luca?* Did he change his mind about waiting to make a decision until after the conclave and tell Franco to take care of the problem of Ana and me now? Was this always his plan?

Or has Franco just completely lost his mind?

"Sit down." He points at one of the chairs. "Do it now!"

I sink into one of the leather chairs, my heart pounding so hard that I can feel it pressing against the walls of my chest. My tongue catches between my teeth as I sit down, and I taste metal in my mouth as I look up at Franco.

"I don't know what you're doing, but Luca—"

"Fuck Luca," he spits. An evil smile crosses his face. "He's weak. You made him weak." His eyes skate over my body lewdly, resting on my breasts before they slide back up to my face. "Normally, I'd have a taste of that sweet pussy for myself. But I don't want to risk it. Fucking bitch. You put some kind of fucking spell on him, I swear. Since you came here, he hasn't been the same."

"He's just in love with me." Saying the words out loud to Franco seems ridiculous. And the look on his face tells me that he thinks the same, as he starts to laugh.

"Luca can't fucking love anyone. He's too afraid of them getting hurt after his dear old dad died because he loved his best friend too much, and then his mother killed herself because she couldn't handle it. Ironic, isn't it? His father died avenging his best friend. Luca's going to die because of his."

"What?" I stare at him, my eyes going round with fear. "Franco, just stop this. Look, I know about what you did. Your deal with the Irish—with your father. I'll find some way to tell Luca it was all a lie. I'll stand up for you, if you just put a stop to this—"

"Liar!" He spits at me, and I feel the hot slide of it down my cheek. "You already betrayed him once. I nearly killed Ana. You think I believe you'd take my side." He laughs then, a deep, rolling laugh that comes from his belly. "Besides, Luca is already dead. That's why I'm here now. I'm going to put you down and then go and finish the other bitch. And then there'll be no one to argue with me when I take Luca's

RUTHLESS PROMISE

seat. It's unfortunate how Viktor turned on Luca at the conclave and killed him, and then my father had to finish Viktor off. Leaves so much territory wide open. But I'm sure my father and I will have a good use for it."

I can feel the cold chill spreading over my skin. *Luca, dead.* It can't be. Grief at the very thought beats at the inside of my chest, clawing at my ribs, threatening to climb up my throat. But if I scream, if I cry, if I let myself give in to it at all, believe it, I won't stop. I'll be hysterical, and that's the last thing I can afford to do right now.

I'm not a damsel in distress. I'm not a princess in a tower, locked away and waiting for someone to come to save her. Luca was never my knight in shining armor.

He was the dragon guarding the tower.

But fuck if I'll let anyone slay my dragon.

I'm not the princess who needs to be rescued anymore.

I'm the fucking queen.

And since Luca's not here to defend his kingdom, I guess I'll have to do it myself.

I hear Franco's finger clicking off the safety of the gun. "Sweet dreams, little Sofia," he says in a singsong voice, sounding almost unhinged, and I dive for the floor, throwing myself to one side of the desk. The shot hits the wood next to me, splintering it, and I feel a fear like I've never experienced wash over me, turning my whole body cold.

Don't freeze up. Don't freeze up.

I need a weapon, something to fight back with. *Surely Luca must have a gun in his office.* I wriggle around behind the desk as another shot goes off, and I hear Franco curse again.

"Just fucking die, bitch!" he screams as I look at the desk, making a split-second decision as to which drawer a gun might be in.

Luca is right-handed. He'd put it in a right-hand drawer. And if he had to get to it quickly? The bottom one, so he could duck down while he grabbed it.

I snatch at the handle of the one I picked, praying it won't be locked. And it's not—clearly, Luca expects that the usually-locked door to the study itself is enough without locking his desk up as well.

The next prayer is that it's loaded. I don't have time to look for bullets, and I sure as fuck don't know how to load a gun. All I know how to do is click off the safety, and as I see another bullet splinter through the desk as Franco fires at me, I know I'm only going to get one chance at this.

I spring up from behind the desk, the gun aimed like I've seen in the movies, one hand clutched under the one holding it as I aim it for Franco's head. I don't have time to think about the implications of what I'm doing or the weight of killing a man. All I know is that he's going to kill me if I don't take him down, and I'm not ready to die.

I pull the trigger.

The shot goes wide. It hits the wall behind Franco, and I only just manage to duck when he shoots again, screaming with frustration. "Just—goddamn it, just die!"

I pop up again from behind the desk, and this time I take one extra second to aim.

It's enough.

"Not today," I whisper. And then I pull the trigger.

This time I don't miss.

The first sensation I have when his body hits the floor is elation, a wild relief that he's down, that he won't have a chance to shoot at me again. And then, as I slowly come around from behind the desk to see if he's still breathing, if I only wounded him, I see very clearly that there's no chance he's still alive.

The wound in his head couldn't be anything other than fatal.

I look at the blood spreading around him, and I can feel nausea taking over. I can't stop myself as I heave, vomit joining the blood on the carpet as I puke my guts up, wave after wave of it coming until I'm on my knees next to the body, shuddering until there's nothing left in me. Even then, I still dry-heave for what seems like forever until I look up and see Ana standing unsteadily in the doorway, her face a mask of pain.

"You shouldn't be standing up," I hear myself say, as if in a tunnel, like I'm outside of my body. "Your feet."

And then everything goes black.

* * *

I WAKE up in the hallway outside of the study, my head in Ana's lap. She's propped up against the wall, stroking my hair as I slowly come back to my senses.

"You shouldn't have gotten out of bed," I whisper, my mouth feeling sticky. "Your feet—"

"There was a gunfight going on," Ana says dryly. "I think in this case, it was warranted."

"How long have I been out?"

"An hour maybe. The security team already came in. Franco had a few guys keeping the cameras off while he tried to take you out, but Raoul and his guys came back and handled them. They're in there with the body now." Ana takes a deep breath, looking down at me. "They called Caterina, too. She's on her way over."

"Oh god," I whisper. The last person I want to see right now is Caterina. I just killed her husband. And while I suspect that she might not cry too many tears over it—I'm still responsible for taking someone else from her after everything else she's been through.

I hear the door opening, and I hope it's just more of the security team coming in. But as footsteps come down the hall, I hear a soft voice call out my name. "Sofia?"

The three of us end up in the living room. Caterina helps me up, and then we both—Caterina more so than I—help Ana make it to the couch. Caterina sinks into one of the chairs, her face pale and drawn. I can see that she's lost weight, a decent bit of it, since the wedding.

"Franco is dead." She says the words simply, quietly, out loud, as if she's telling herself. "They said you shot him, Sofia."

I nod, my throat closing over so that at first I feel like I can't speak. "He was going to kill me."

Caterina nods slowly, her hands on her knees, her knuckles

turning white as she grips them. "They said that too," she whispers. "They offered to show me the tape, but I believed them. You wouldn't kill anyone without cause. And besides—" she pushes up the sleeves of her shirt then, and Ana and I both gasp as we see the bruises on her forearms, reaching up past her elbows.

"He hasn't been kind to anyone lately," she says softly. "Thank god I'm not pregnant."

Ana shifts uncomfortably, and Caterina looks over at her, her keen eyes taking in the expression on Ana's face. "Did he do that to you?" She nods at Ana's bare, bandaged feet, her swollen eyes, her bruised and split lips, and nearly-broken nose.

A moment passes, and Ana hesitates, but she finally nods. "He found out that I was trying to help Sofia leave. But he also wanted me dead because I discovered his plot to kill Luca and Viktor and Sofia and take over the territory with the help of his father."

Caterina's eyes widen. "His father? His father is dead—"

"His father is Colin Macgregor," I interject. "The rumors are true. They were plotting to do away with the Russians and Italians and take all of the Northeast territories for themselves."

"Fuck," Caterina whispers. "Oh god—Luca?"

I shake my head. "I don't know. I haven't heard anything. Franco said he was already dead, but—" I want to say *I'd know if he was*, but that sounds like so much new age-y bullshit.

I just can't let myself believe it. Because if he's dead—

Then the last thing we ever did was fight. The last words he ever said to me were a threat to kill me.

Then he'll never know about our baby. Never know how I feel about him. Never know that I want to fix it all, every argument and unkind word and betrayal and lie.

He'll never know I love him or that I know he loves me too.

"He can't be," I whisper. "He just can't."

Caterina looks at me curiously. "Why were you trying to leave?" she asks evenly, and I can hear the reason for the question in her voice. If I betrayed Luca just to get out of my marriage, I don't think

I'll find much sympathy with her. I know I have to tell her the truth. The first person other than Ana that I've told.

"I'm pregnant," I say simply.

"I don't understand."

I explain the terms of the contract to her, my voice tired and drained, and I see Caterina's eyes go wide with horror as she listens.

"Sofia, I can't—I don't know why he would do that. Why he would make you promise something so awful. But I can't believe that if he knew, he'd make you go through with it." She pauses, rubbing her hands on her legs as she looks between the two of us. "Sofia, if he comes back from the conclave alive, you have to tell him. You have to trust him with that. Trust that he'll do the right thing." She looks at Ana. "Don't you agree?"

"Weirdly enough, I do." Ana looks at me from where she's lying on the couch, her feet gingerly elevated. "I think Luca loves you. I just think he doesn't know the first fucking way to tell you. So maybe this will be your bridge back to each other."

"I agree," Caterina says softly.

I sit there between the two women, one of them mired in grief for her family, one of them for the life she's lost now because of the other's now-dead husband. I feel myself tottering on edge too. The only thing that keeps me from tumbling over is the fact that I don't really know if Luca is dead or not.

I have hope. Hope that he's still alive, hope that he'll come home, hope that we can repair all of this. Hope that he'll be happy about our child.

It's not much. But it's kept me going before.

I look up and see Raoul and three of his men carrying Franco's shrouded body down on a stretcher. Caterina is watching them, her face pale and still, her eyes clear. No tears from her, and I can't blame her.

But I feel my stomach twist with fear because it's all too easy to imagine my own husband underneath a shroud like that, being carried back to me.

Just come home, Luca. Please come home.

LUCA

21

At first, I'm pretty sure the light above me is the proverbial light at the end of the tunnel. And then my eyes open a little wider, and I realize that it's the fluorescent bulbs of the hospital.

I'm alive, somehow.

It comes as a shock. I'd really believed that was the end of the line, that the last thing I'd ever see was that paisley hotel carpet in front of my eyes.

But I can hear the beeping of the machines, feel the stiff pain in my side when I move. I'm shirtless, my side wrapped in gauze, and I can feel that it takes some effort to breathe deeply. "Pretty sure something in there got real fucked up," I mutter underneath my breath, looking at the bruised flesh around the gauze.

"You're right fucked up," a deep, Irish-accented voice next to me says, and I flinch hard, my vision clearing entirely as I snap to full attention.

Colin Macgregor is sitting next to my bed, a gun in his hand.

"Shame," he says, shaking his head. "I used to be a better shot than that. But you know, old age and all that. It comes to us all."

"What happened—" I croak out, my throat and mouth so dry I can barely speak. "Viktor—"

"I put him in the hospital too, I'm afraid, but not quite dead yet. I'll be paying him a visit soon, don't worry, lad. His second is headed six feet under as soon as they can bury him."

"Liam?" I feel a sharp pang of worry for the boy, who was brave enough to stand up to his father in front of everyone.

"Aye, he's due a good beating. But I'm not one to kill my own flesh and blood." He leans forward, the gun still casually held in his hand. "I've got other marks to finish off first, anyway. You, for one, Luca Romano." He grins, his aged face wrinkling as he does. "I'm not sure what to do with your wife, to be honest. I hear she's right turned your head with that sweet quim in between her legs. So maybe I'll have a taste before I end her, aye? Or maybe I should keep her for my own. A nice little side piece to warm my bed when I feel like having something besides the old lady in my bed?"

"Don't you fucking touch Sofia," I hiss. "I swear to god, Colin Macgregor."

"Aye, swear to him." He stands up, his grip tightening on the gun. "You'll be meeting him soon enough."

I can feel the cold pit of fear in my belly, for all my bravado. I escaped once, but there's no missing now. He's too close, with no other distractions. This isn't him shooting me across a table, with his son doing his best to stop his father from a rash action. This is him, alone and confident, and I know my time has come.

My number's up, as they say. And I guess I won't get to say the words to Sofia after all.

I tried to protect you. I tried—

"Say goodnight, lad." Colin presses the barrel to my forehead, and I close my eyes, refusing to show him even an ounce of fear. I'll die well, at least, if I have to die.

The crack of the gunshot reverberates through my body, an electric jolt of pain crashing through me as my body reacts to it, jerking in the bed, a hot wash of pain joining it as the wound in my stomach protests.

A scream echoes in the room, and there's the sound of a body crashing into something metallic and then hitting the floor.

A moment later, I pry one eye open, and then the other, and I realize that despite my body's reaction to the shot, I'm not dead at all.

The gunshot wasn't Colin's.

I look over to see one of my bodyguards, Val, walking into the room, his gun clutched hard in one hand. "Are you alright, boss?" he asks, his voice tight. "I got the fucker, I think."

Slowly, I look to the other side, seeing Colin's body on the floor, blood spreading across the tile. He's not dead, the shot hit him square in the side, but he's unconscious, slumped against the radiator on the wall.

"Yes," I say in a voice that doesn't sound quite like my own. "I think you did."

***

It's a week before they allow me to fly home. In that time, I don't call Sofia. I want to speak to her in person the next time she hears my voice because there's a lot to say still, and I'm not sure what decision I want to make yet.

I'm not going to have her killed, obviously. I'd said that in anger, it's not possible that I could do that. Especially not with our baby in her belly. But beyond that—

Can I trust her now, after everything? More importantly, can I *love* her? Can I raise a family with her?

I don't know the answers to those questions. And I need time to think. I can't have a woman by my side that I can't trust, no matter how much I want her. Passion, desire, and even love aren't enough to make a relationship work in my world. I know that much.

What matters in the end, besides trust, is if Sofia *wants* to be a part of this world, this life, with me. And the only way I know to find that out is to give her the opportunity to tell me the truth and see what happens.

The penthouse is very quiet when I walk in. I'm moving slowly, still with a limp from the healing wound in my stomach, and I make my way through the lower floor, looking for my wife. I avoid the study—I know what happened there now. The rugs and floor will have been cleaned, but I'm still not prepared quite yet to look at the spot where my best friend died, the man who betrayed me more deeply than I imagined anyone ever could. The Abel to my Cain, my brother.

And now he's gone.

I don't want to lose anyone else. My chest tightens as I make my way slowly upstairs. Sofia isn't in her room; when I crack the door, I see Ana lying on top of that bed, a throw blanket over her as she naps. I step back out into the hall quietly, knowing there's only one other place Sofia could be.

She's in our bedroom, sitting on the edge of the bed with her hands pressed between her knees. She doesn't look up when I walk in.

"I heard you were coming home today," she says softly. "I'm glad you're alive."

"Are you?" I can't help but ask; it's an honest question. If I were dead, she'd be free. I'm reminded of us having a very similar conversation in the hospital after the hotel was attacked. Then, Rossi was still alive and very much a danger to her. Now, if I were gone, there would be no one left to keep her here. Viktor has no use for her anymore. "You'd be able to leave if I were dead."

"I don't want you dead." Her voice is quiet, flat, as if she's holding back her emotion. "I mean it. I'm glad you're safe."

"What about you?" I don't make a move to walk further into the room yet, staying just inside the door as I close it behind me. "Are you alright?"

"As much as I can be. I killed a man." Her voice is still toneless and low. "My first time."

"The first time is always the hardest."

"He tried to kill me first."

"I know. They told me everything. I don't blame you, Sofia."

"Do you know everything?" She's still not looking at me. "What he did?"

"I do," I confirm. "Viktor filled me in on his treachery. I would have done it myself if you hadn't. After what he did to Ana—"

"He was hurting Caterina, too. She showed me the bruises."

"Shit." I grit my teeth, a fresh wave of rage towards a dead man washing over me. "He got what he deserved, Sofia. You shouldn't feel guilty."

"I don't. I don't feel much of anything."

"I was wrong about Franco," I say slowly, taking another step into the room. "I trusted him, and I was wrong. And now I wonder what else I was wrong about. I trusted you, and you plotted with Ana to betray me."

"So, are you going to have me killed?"

"No, Sofia," I say quietly. "But I think maybe, now that the Bratva threat is gone and Franco is dead, it might be time to go back to what we originally agreed. I'll arrange for you to have an apartment of your own. We can live separately, even divorce if that's what you want, when things have calmed down." *Like hell will I divorce you,* I think even as I say it, but I need her to believe me. I need to know if she'll tell me the truth when given a chance if she'll fight back.

If she wants to stay.

"You can go to Paris," I continue. "You can still have your career. I'll talk to the director at Juilliard and arrange for you to finish your classes to graduate. You can go back to your life now, Sofia. The danger is gone. So I suppose our marriage is no longer necessary."

There's a long silence that stretches out between us, and I wonder if she's going to come clean after all or if she's going to keep her secrets. And if she does, what do I do then?

And then, finally, she turns towards me and looks at me for the first time since I walked into the room, and says the words that I've been waiting to hear.

"Luca, I'm pregnant."

SOFIA

22

I feel as if my heart is going to pound out of my chest.

He gave me an out. An escape. I could have taken it. I could have kept the baby a secret and accepted his offer to leave. Been in Paris by the time I gave birth. Gone to London.

Never come back to Manhattan again.

Leave this all behind.

Not too long ago, that would have been everything I'd hoped and prayed for. But now I know for sure that it's not what I want anymore. I don't want to live apart from my husband, and I don't want to leave.

I've killed for him. And now I'm ready to fight for him. For *us*.

"How long have you known?" Luca's voice is careful, taut, and I can't tell if he's happy or not.

I get up from the bed slowly and walk towards him. He doesn't move, and I can see him swallow hard, his Adam's apple bobbing in his throat.

"I knew the day you came home bloody," I say quietly. "The day you were angry at me for going to the hospital with Caterina. I'd been sick, but I thought it was just some kind of stomach flu. And then I got into an argument with Rossi, and he tore my necklace off, and I vomited in the bathroom. The next day I was still sick, and I realized I'd missed my period. I knew then," I continue, breathing in deeply, "but they confirmed it at the hospital after you brought me there."

"And you didn't tell me?"

"I couldn't." My voice is soft, pleading. "Luca, you made me sign that awful contract, saying that I'd terminate if I ever got pregnant. I didn't know why that clause was in there when I signed, and I didn't think it would matter. I didn't even think we'd have sex, let alone—" my voice catches. I have to breathe in again, trying desperately to keep control of my emotions. "I didn't know what to do. After the way you were that night, I felt so far away from you, so scared. I didn't know if you'd make me stick to it or not, and I wanted the baby. I couldn't do it. And even if you'd been happy about it, I was afraid of that, too. Afraid of the life you'd raise the baby in, afraid of what would happen if we had a boy, even more afraid of what would happen if we had a girl. I remembered my father dying and leaving my mother and me alone, and I was afraid that might happen to you, that our child could lose his or her father if someone killed you. There's so much danger in this life, so much—"

My voice catches again, and I have to choke back the rising tears—tears of fear, tears of sadness, tears of grief, because I'm almost certain from the impassive way that Luca's looking at me that he's *not* happy, that he doesn't want the baby, or me. That everything I'd hoped for is gone. That at best, I'll have to leave.

At worst, I'll lose my baby.

"I don't understand," I say softly. "Why you would make me get rid of our baby."

"Rossi, Franco, and I had an agreement," Luca says simply. "Before it became necessary for me to marry you. I was supposed to be don until Franco had a son of age, and then I was meant to pass the title on to him. That's why Franco and Caterina were engaged. So that some of Rossi's blood would continue in the title. I was only ever meant to be a placeholder. And when our marriage became necessary, it was expected that would still happen—which meant we couldn't have children."

"Oh." It's a simple explanation, but it makes sense—in the minds of the men who run this family, at least. "Well, I guess that doesn't matter now." I lick my lips, wrapping my arms around myself. "Franco is dead, and Caterina isn't pregnant."

"I know."

"I can't stay with someone who would have forced me to do that." It's hard for me to say those words, but I know that I have to. I need to hear him say that he wants our baby. If I can't hear that from him, then I know there's nothing left for us.

"Sofia." Luca looks down at me, and I see his face soften for the first time since he walked into the room. "I knew about the baby before our honeymoon."

"What?" I stare at him, stunned. "And you didn't say anything? Why?"

"I wanted to give you the opportunity to tell me yourself," he says simply.

"I almost did, so many times—" I trail off, thinking of all the times I nearly came clean. "I was so scared, though."

"I thought when I had that contract written up that I could do that easily," he continues. "I'd never been in a relationship. Hardly ever slept with the same woman more than once. The idea of a real marriage, of partnership, of love, of a family, of being a *father* was so alien to me that I couldn't possibly imagine it happening. I couldn't see anything that would change the path I was on. So it didn't seem all that difficult to me to agree to that. To maintain the legacy that Rossi wanted."

He takes a step closer to me then, his eyes darkening as his gaze meets mine. "But once I knew, Sofia, once it was *real*, I knew I couldn't. I wanted our baby, too. I wanted *you*. That's why I put so much effort into the 'honeymoon.' I wanted to see if we could work. If my feelings were real, and I wanted you to tell me. But the truth was that I couldn't fathom letting our baby go, or you. But then—" his jaw tightens. "We came home, and I found out that you and Ana were plotting for you to run."

"Luca, surely you understand—"

"I do," he interrupts. "I do understand why you did it, why you felt so desperate. And I forgive you, Sofia. But if we have any chance at this, any chance at all—we have to tell each other the truth. We have to be honest." He takes a deep breath, and for the first time since he came into the room, he touches me.

His fingers trail beneath my chin, and I shiver at his touch.

"I found your journal," I whisper. "Was it real? What you wrote?"

Luca's gaze holds mine, and I see something there, a deep, fathomless emotion. "Yes," he murmurs, his voice low and smoky. "All of it."

"And do you still mean it? What if I say I want to stay?" The words tumble out of my lips, quick and nervous. "What if—"

"You have to be all in, Sofia. With me, with this life. There are no half-measures here. Desire and love aren't enough. You have to want my world if you want me. We can do this together, or not at all. But there's no other way."

My breath catches in my throat, my pulse speeding up. His hand is still on my jaw, holding my face gently, but I see something darker in his gaze. It's not anger. It's possessiveness, that old familiar need.

I'm his. But he needs to know that I believe that, too.

"What happens now?" I whisper. "Now that Franco is dead, now that the Irish betrayed you? What happens with Viktor?"

"There's peace with the Bratva now. Viktor had one condition—Colin Macgregor's life." A small muscle in Luca's cheek jumps as his jaw clenches. "It was a condition I was happy to grant. He's being held hostage now, and we'll take care of that particular problem soon, once Viktor is out of the hospital."

"So we'll be at war with the Irish?" My voice trembles, although I don't want it to.

"No." Luca's voice is firm. "Colin's son Liam stood against him at the conclave. He'll inherit, and he'll keep the peace. He understands why his father's punishment is what it is. He won't argue with it." Luca is silent for a moment, looking at my expression. "This is our way, Sofia. It's the way things are. You need to understand that if you're going to stay. If you're going to be at my side. It's a hard life and a brutal one at times." His hand strokes my cheek, his knuckles brushing over the high line of my cheekbone.

"But it's a beautiful one sometimes, too."

I reach up, covering his hand with mine. "I don't want to leave." I meet his eyes, my voice strong and steady now. "I knew how I felt when I found your journal. And then when Franco tried to kill me—" I take a deep breath, my gaze fixed on his. Strong, unfaltering. The way I always hope to be. "I found something inside of myself that I didn't know was there. I didn't just want to save my own life. I wanted to protect you, too. Our home. Our life. I wasn't going to let him tear it all down. And that's when I knew that I was in the right place."

Slowly, I step forward until my body is almost brushing his. "I didn't think I wanted this life," I whisper. "I didn't understand why my father gave me to you, knowing the kind of man you were. Bloody, violent, angry. But now—now I understand. Because you are those things, but you're more, too."

When his hands close on my upper arms, pulling me against him, I feel the rush of desire overwhelm me, my body melting into his as I reach up, twining my arms around his neck.

When his lips come down on mine, I feel like I'm coming home.

And when we tumble back onto the bed, his hands stripping away my clothes as I do the same to him, I know that I'll never want to leave again.

Luca's hands run over my face, my breasts, down my waist to my hips as I spread my legs for him, wrapping them around his hips as he angles himself against my already wet core, sliding the tip of his cock into me and holding himself there, looking down at me with that dark, smoky gaze.

"Mine," he whispers, pushing forward another inch.

"My wife." Another inch, and I gasp, feeling my body stretch around him, feeling his thick hardness fill me.

"My queen." Another, and I moan, tilting my chin up, but he doesn't kiss me yet.

"My love."

He slides into me fully, sinking to the hilt, and I cry out, my body winding around his as he begins to thrust, and my hips rise with each stroke, meeting him again and again.

"I love you," I whisper against his mouth as he kisses me, his hands cupping my face, his body slowly moving within me. I can feel him straining to hold back, and my desire crests again, reaching its peak as he presses his forehead against mine. "Come with me," I whisper. "I'm going to come, Luca, come with me, baby—"

"Fuck!" He groans as he feels me tighten around him, my hips arching so that I'm pressed against him, every inch of him against every part of me. I hear him whisper as I feel him thrust once more, his hips bucking as his orgasm spills into me, joining with mine.

"I love you," he whispers. "Sofia. I love you, I love you. I'll never let you go."

He rolls onto his side, bringing me with him, holding me in his arms. "You're mine," he murmurs softly, stroking my hair, still half-buried inside of me. "Mine, forever."

"I'll never leave again." I brush my fingers over his forehead. "I trust you, Luca. I know you'll keep us safe. And I'm ready to be in this world with you. I'm not afraid anymore."

He kisses the top of my head, laying back against the pillows with me still cradled in his arms. "When you said earlier that I was more," he asks, his green eyes meeting mine. "What did you mean?"

I smile softly, nestling into him as I press my hand against his chest, bringing his to mine as I feel his heart beating beneath my palm. "You're not just the hard man you were raised to be," I say softly. "You're so many other things, too."

"Like what?" Luca's eyes crinkle softly with humor. "Tell me, wife."

"Brave," I whisper. "Loyal. Fair. Relentless in the pursuit of what you want. Charming. Charismatic. Ambitious."

I look up at him, into the eyes of the man I want to spend the rest of my life with, and I know at last, with absolute certainty, that I've made the right choice.

"And when it comes to the ones you love? Ruthless."

EPILOGUE

LUCA

The meeting takes place in my office.

It's the first time I've been here since Franco was killed. There's an ache in my chest when I realize that he won't be taking his place in the chair on the other side of my desk, that he won't lazily slouch there, pretending not to give a shit about any of this.

That not only is my best friend gone forever, but his memory is tainted beyond all redemption.

The door opens, and Viktor and Liam walk in. The latter's face is pale and sober, but he's well-dressed in a charcoal suit, his shoulders squared and his back straight.

I stand and meet them in front of my desk, shaking their hands in turn. There's a solemn, heavy air in the room, and we all know why that is.

Liam, surprisingly, is the one to break the silence.

"I understand why it had to be done," he says, his voice quiet but firm. "I didn't know about my father's betrayal, nor Franco's. I didn't even know I had a half-brother." A shadow of grief passes over his face then, but he doesn't falter. He stands firm, a man despite his relative youth. "If I had known, I would have stopped it long before it got that far." He looks at us both, his gaze resolute. "I want peace, as much as anyone."

Viktor reaches into his pocket then and holds out his hand. "For you," he says simply, and when Liam opens his palm, Viktor places Colin's ring into it, the emerald signet that he always wore.

Liam's hand closes around it, making a tight fist as it falls to his side.

"Your father died bravely," Viktor says, looking at Liam squarely. "It was quick, and he went without complaint and with honor. We'll return the body to your family for burial."

"Thank you." Liam's voice is rarely accented, but I hear a trace of it as the grief thickens his speech.

"Is that enough for peace?" I look at Viktor. "Franco Bianchi is dead. Colin Macgregor is dead. The betrayal is finished, the plot undone. Are you agreeable that it's enough?"

Viktor turns to look at me fully. "Franco was like your brother," he says, his voice stiff. "He was your underboss, your right hand. And yet, you could not control him. He allied himself with me against you, and he betrayed me. He broke his promise to us. So I would ask for one more thing, to keep the peace. The last thing he can do, even in death, to make this right."

I frown. "What? If it's in my power to give, I'm happy to. I want this to be done."

A slow smile spreads across Viktor's face. "I want his widow," he says simply.

"I want Caterina Rossi as my wife."

* * *

THANK you for reading the Promise Series. Want to continue the journey following Caterina? Order Captive Bride here. Continue reading for a sneak peak.

CATERINA

1

*E*very mafia bride knows that there may be a day when she has to dress for her husband's funeral.

This is a dangerous life we all lead, after all, especially the men. This is a world of blood and violence, riches and excess paid for with short, fast lives that burn hot and bright and flame out just as quickly. I've always thought that was probably one of the reasons why love so rarely factors into mafia marriages.

It's easier to see a black dress hanging side by side in your closet with your wedding gown if the marriage is made for convenience, and not love.

I hadn't loved Franco. Not in the way that most people think of love. There was nothing of romance novels in our relationship, very little in the way of passion. The roses and jewelry and grand gestures were because they were expected, not because he was madly in love with me. I was—am—a mafia princess, after all. Courting me meant pulling out all the stops, even if the eventual decision about my marriage hadn't really been in my hands at all.

It had been in my father's hands, and I had always known that was how things would be.

My father.

It's my late husband's fault that my father is dead. That my mother is dead. That I'm standing here in front of the full-length mirror in my childhood room, my knee-length black dress still unzipped, the tulle of the half-veil I'm expected to wear to the funeral crushed in my hands. This is the third funeral I will have gone to in nearly as many months. The third funeral of someone close to me, no less.

How much is one person supposed to take before she breaks?

Gingerly, I touch my forearm. My dress is long-sleeved, not because of the weather but because of the yellowing bruises running up and down my arms like grotesque bracelets. Franco left his hands off of my neck and face, at least, although not all the other parts of my body were so lucky. And it's less than he did to poor Anastasia, at least. He knew at least enough to keep the evidence from the one other man left who would have been furious to know that Franco had laid hands on me.

Luca Romano. My father's heir. My late husband's supposed best friend. The don of the Northeast chapter of the American mafia.

And now, my only possible protector. I am a woman without a close living male relative, without a husband, and in the world I live in, that's a dangerous, vulnerable position to be in. Even my status as a mafia princess, the only daughter of the late former don, won't save me from any number of possible unfortunate fates if I don't have someone to look out for me. If anything, it makes my position even more tenuous. I'm a valuable hostage, an excellent bargaining chip, a coveted bride despite being newly widowed.

But I hope that Luca will protect me from all of that. I'll be able to come back here, to the home I grew up in that now belongs to me, and grieve in peace. Not for Franco—I can't feel much grief for him after what he did—to my family, to Luca, to Sofia, to Ana. But I'm still grieving for my parents, and now I'm grieving something else.

The life I'd thought I would have.

Slowly, I cross the room to the closet, ostensibly to get my shoes—sensible black pumps with a pointed toe and short heel, nothing too provocative. But next to my shoes is a long flat box, and I know what's inside of it.

My wedding dress.

I know there's no point in looking backwards. But I can't stop myself from cracking the lid anyway, reaching inside to touch the cool satin. Sofia Romano, Luca's wife, helped me pick that dress out, only a few days after my mother died. She was a good friend to me when I needed one most, when I was jolted out of my grief into a hastier wedding than expected to keep me safe from Viktor Andreyev, the leader of the Bratva here in Manhattan. And Franco tried to kill her. He tried to kill *Luca*.

So no, I won't grieve for him.

But what I *am* grieving for is the man I thought he was. The carefree, laughing, red-headed, boyish man who my father chose for me. I'd known him already, of course. He'd been Luca's closest friend since childhood, and Luca's father had been close to mine. We'd all grown up together. I'd thought he was handsome, if reckless and a little childish. More boy than man, always. I'd never imagined he would be my husband. But I hadn't been upset that he'd been chosen for me, either. It could have been much worse—or so I'd thought at the time, anyway.

I'd always been aware of what the circumstances of my eventual marriage would be. I'd always known that whoever I married would be someone who benefited my father. I'd come to terms with that long before my engagement. It was why I'd never really dated, even though it wasn't expressly forbidden. There was no point, in my mind. Why date, when I knew I would have no choice in my future husband? Why put temptation in my way, when I knew that my virginity was a precious commodity, and not my own to give away as I pleased?

The most sensible thing to do was to not torture myself with crushes and flings that could never be anything more.

And I've always been nothing if not sensible.

But what that meant was that Franco was my first kiss. My first everything. I'd thrown myself headlong into the relationship after our engagement, wanting to please him. I'd expected him to stray—I knew very well that almost all mafia husbands did. But I'd wanted to delay his eventual unfaithfulness as long as I could. *I went down on him in a limo just after he proposed to me, for fuck's sake.*

The bitterness of the thought startles me. I hadn't expected close emotional intimacy between us, or faithfulness, or even real love. I'd thought that I'd been as practical as I possibly could about what our marriage would be. But I *had* expected some things.

I'd been thrilled that my father had chosen someone my own age. Someone fun and full of life. Someone who didn't take things quite as seriously as so many of the other men around me. I'd seen Franco as, if not a devoted partner, an adventure. Someone that could maybe help me cut loose a little, lighten up. Someone that I could have fun with, laugh with, enjoy being with. Someone who would be an adventurous lover, someone who I could unashamedly explore all the things I'd always been curious about in bed with. A friend, maybe.

Very, very briefly, I'd thought that I'd had that. Our first nights together had been good, even if he'd seemed slightly frustrated by my inexperience. My virginity hadn't seem so much a turn-on to him as an annoyance, but I'd told myself that was good. At least he wasn't the type of man to fetishize virginity. We hadn't gotten a honeymoon, but we'd gotten a few days to hide away in my family home, and I'd done my best to be a happy new bride, even at a time when I was also a grieving daughter.

But Franco had had no patience for that. And our relationship had devolved quickly. I'd seen his irritation, his impatience, his lack of caring for me almost immediately. I'd realized very soon that I was a stepping stone for him, nothing more. That he hadn't had any hopes for our marriage other than to hope that I wouldn't be too much trouble.

That hurt. But everything that followed hurt so much more. And the revelations that came with his death?

Those nearly broke me.

I pull my hand back from the box, pushing the lid shut as I grab my shoes and stand up, slipping them on quickly. Sofia told me to take as much time as I needed, but I know I'll need to emerge sooner rather than later. It wouldn't do for the widow to be late to her own husband's funeral.

There's a knock at the door, and I lick my dry lips, my mouth feeling cottony. "Come in," I call out, my voice cracking slightly as I turn to get my mother's pearls from my jewelry box. Next to them, my extravagant engagement ring glitters in the light, and I snatch the pearls up, shutting the box before I succumb to the urge to grab it and throw it across the room. I wish I could take off all the evidence that I was ever married to him at all, but it would be absolutely scandalous to show up without so much as a wedding band on. Leaving my ostentatious ring off will seem like a show of modesty, but a bare hand would be whispered about for months.

Sofia told me that Luca's done his best to keep the extent of what Franco and Franco's father—his *real* father—did quiet, containing it to the upper levels of the mafia, Bratva, and Irish hierarchies. It's better for it to not spread too widely. It's too insidious, too great of a lie and too large of a betrayal to let the lesser men know about. It might give others ideas, if they knew how long Franco and his father managed to hide it all, how close they came to bringing down an entire family and their heirs.

"Caterina?" Sofia Romano, my closest friend now—especially after everything that's happened—steps into the room. She's wearing a simple black dress, high-necked and knee-length, with elbow-length sleeves and her dark hair pulled back into a smooth bun. It's very similar to the one I have on, but there's one very noticeable difference between our silhouettes—Sofia's stomach is faintly rounded, the slightest hint of her pregnancy starting to show. It's just barely there, if I hadn't known, I might just have thought she'd had a large breakfast. But I know—I was the one who encouraged her to tell her husband.

Sofia and I have had each other's backs for some time now. And I don't expect that to change anytime soon.

It's a relief to have one person that I feel I can lean on. Two really, if I count Luca, but I'm not certain that I can yet. I haven't spoken to him since Franco's death, or since he came back from the hospital. I think Sofia would have warned me if Luca blamed me in any way, or if he intended to hold me responsible for my husband's crimes as well, but I still can't help but be afraid. Luca has never been as cruel, harsh, or commanding as most mafia men are—men like my late father. But the title of don, the responsibility of it, changes men. My mother told me that. And Luca has never been a particularly warm man, either. He's always been kind to me, but I don't yet know if he'll put the mafia first, or my happiness and safety.

I hope it's the latter.

I simply want to be left alone to grieve, for the first time since my parents' deaths. I intend to square things with Luca today, after the funeral, and then hopefully I'll be allowed to retreat, into my own private sanctuary, a convent of one. I have no desire to remarry, or to even really take part in this life anymore.

If I could disappear altogether, I think I would.

This life has taken far too much from me already.

"Are you alright?" Sofia looks at me sympathetically. "I know, that's a loaded question. Here, let me do up your zipper for you." She comes to stand behind me, gently tugging up the zipper and smoothing her hands down the back of my dress so that the crisp fabric lays correctly. I look painfully thin, far more than I ever have been, although I've always been slender. My cheekbones look as if they're pushing at my chin, my jawline sharp, my eyes tired. Even a generous helping of mascara and concealer couldn't hide the fact that I haven't slept in what feels like months. Once a man lays hands on you, it's difficult to sleep well next to him any longer. But sleeping in another bedroom was never an option for me. Neither was telling Franco no, when he required my attentions in bed. He'd wanted me to produce an heir for him as quickly as possible, to solidify that hopeful son's eventual rise to the seat that my father, and now Luca, occupied.

I touch my stomach surreptitiously, letting out a sigh of relief for the thousandth time that I didn't get pregnant over the course of our short marriage. Sofia is glowing with her pregnancy, and in the brief time that I'd had some happiness with Franco, I'd imagined myself the same way—radiant and happy to be having his child.

Now I can't imagine it. Not just Franco's, but anyone's. I've always loved children, but the life of a mafia wife and mother feels light years away now, as if a different woman tried to live it.

I'm done with men. I never expected love, but the thought of marriage, of being a trophy on someone's arm, of sex, makes me feel sick now.

If I have my way, I'll never be married again.

"You don't have to do anything," Sofia tells me gently, resting a hand on my elbow. "Everyone expects you to be grieving. Just you being there is all you need to do." She reaches for my hand, taking the crumpled half-veil out of it and reaching up to pin it into my hair, smoothed back into a carefully pinned twist.

"Won't I need to say something? A eulogy for my husband?" I lick my lips nervously, looking at my reflection. I *look* as if I'm carrying the heavy weight of grief, because I am, even if not for Franco. But I don't know how I'll get up behind a podium and look out across the gathered mourners, most of whom aren't even aware of Franco's betrayal, and give a eulogy appropriate for a grieving widow for a man that I now hate.

A man that, if I really look into the deepest, darkest corners of my soul, I'm glad is dead.

"I've already told Luca to take point on that," Sofia says firmly, clipping the other corner of the veil into my hair. The black tulle covers my eyes down to the pointed tip of my nose, giving me an appropriately elegant air, and most importantly, hiding how truly awful I look these days. I'm a long way from my homecoming queen days, from being the most beautiful girl not just among the mafia daughters, but maybe even in greater Manhattan. I'd always been aware of how pretty I was, maybe even a little vain about it. I'm sure it will return in time, though I'm no longer interested in what I can buy with that currency. But today at least, I look much older than my twenty-two years.

"So I don't have to speak at all?" I glance sideways at her. "Won't everyone think that's strange?"

"When he asks you to come up, just start to go, and then break down crying. Fake it if you need to," Sofia says encouragingly. "And he'll say something about how heartbroken you are, and Father Donahue will move things along."

I let out a breath that I hadn't known I was holding. "Thank you," I whisper, turning to face her and grasping her hands in mine. I can feel tears gathering at the corners of my eyes. "Thank you for being here for me, through all of this. I know it hasn't been easy for you."

"It hasn't," Sofia admits. "But it's better now—for me, for Luca. We're better. We're finding our way through all of this. And you will too, Caterina, I promise. Things will get better."

She reaches up underneath my veil, brushing a tear off of my cheek with her thumb. "Franco is dead. He can't hurt you, or anyone, anymore. You'll heal from all of this. You just need time. Just get through today, and then you'll have all the time you need to grieve, and heal, and find out who you want to be. Just a few more hours, and by tonight, it will all be over."

I cling to that, as I pick up my purse and rosary and follow Sofia out of the bedroom, out to the waiting car.

By tonight, it will all be over.

I can put all of this behind me, and start fresh, as my own woman.

Caterina Rossi, a free woman.

It has a nice ring to it.

CATERINA

2

I keep repeating that over and over, like a prayer or a mantra, all the way down the aisle of the cathedral to my seat in the front pew. I force myself not to think of how, not that long ago, I walked down this same aisle all in white, with Franco waiting at the altar for me. How hopeful I'd been, that day! I'd managed my expectations, but I'd still had hope for some happiness. For a good marriage, by mafia standards.

Now I'm walking to my seat all in black, the gold band on my left ring finger burning into my skin like a brand, one that I can't wait to take off. It'll be the first thing I do, once everyone is gone tonight and I'm alone again.

Everyone wants to comfort me, to tell me how sorry they are, to share how shocked and heartbroken they are at Franco's death. It's all I can do to nod and force myself through it, when all I want to do is scream that he wasn't the man that they—or I—thought he was. That he was a traitor, a murderer, that he deserved worse than he got. I picture the horrified looks on their faces if I told them the truth—if I told them about the way he tortured Ana, ruining her dancer's feet forever, or the way he'd punched me in the stomach the first time I got my period after our wedding, or rolled up my sleeve to show the bruises from only a few days ago. If I told them how he'd held me down, ordering me to shut up when I told him that I hadn't been in the mood for sex one night not more than a month after we'd been married.

When you give me a son, you can claim you have a headache all you want. Until then, spread your legs and shut up, princess. That's all you were ever good for, anyway.

Do your duty. I'd heard my mother's voice in my head that night. She would have told me to get it over with, that the sooner I was pregnant the sooner he'd leave me alone. *Men don't like sleeping with their pregnant wives,* she'd have told me. *They'll find someone else to keep them company, and you'll be happy about it.*

My mother had been very good at managing my expectations, when it came to my future husband. But there's no way she could have prepared me for what Franco turned out to be.

Finally, I make my way to my seat, clenching my hands together in my lap, forcing myself to look down at them as I wait for Father Donahue to make his way to the podium, to start the service. I don't look at the gleaming casket, surrounded by flowers, or the photos of Franco, smiling boyishly out from the frames. I especially don't look at the one of us on our wedding day, the same hands that are wrapped together in my lap right now clasped in his. I know what photo it is. In it, I'm looking up at him, and he's looking at me. When I first saw it, I thought the possessive look in his eyes was romantic. Now, I know that it's psychotic.

It's the look of a man who sees the path to power and influence in front of him. Not a wife, not a lover. A ladder.

"Brothers and sisters, we are gathered here today to mourn the passing of one of our own, Franco Bianchi." Father Donahue's voice, thick and rich with Irish brogue, pulls me out of my thoughts. Sofia's hand finds its way to mine, covering them, and I look up, startled. I hadn't even realized she'd sat down next to me, Luca on the other side.

Carefully, I loosen my hands, letting her slip hers between them. It feels good, to have a friend holding my hand. Comforting. It makes me think, just for a moment, that perhaps she was right. That if I can just get through this, the funeral and the reception afterwards, everything will be okay. I can grieve on my own, alone, in my own way. I can put all of this behind me, and start anew. I can decide, for the first time in my life, who Caterina Rossi ought to be.

I hardly hear the rest of the service. I don't really hear Father Donahue give the floor to Luca, and I'm barely aware of what Luca says, some manufactured speech about how Franco was like a brother to him, how unexpected his death was, how tragic. Those closest to Luca know the truth, of course, but the rest of the sea of mourners in the cathedral will simply be nodding along, dabbing away tears with handkerchiefs, touched by Luca's entirely fabricated eulogy.

I almost miss Luca calling me up to give my own. Sofia's hand on my back helps me to stand, but I have a sudden rush of memory—standing up to speak at my mother's funeral not all that long ago, and then my father's just after that, and the grief that rises up to choke me and make itself known in a splutter of sobs isn't fake at all. It's real, and I clap my hand over my mouth, sinking back into the pew as Sofia's arm goes around my shoulders, supporting me.

Distantly, I hear Luca making apologies for me, the grief-stricken widow. There's a hum of sympathy, and Father Donahue moves things along just as Sofia and I had planned, but I'm crying in earnest now, mascara tears running down my cheeks.

I manage to pull myself together as we head out to the cemetery. I feel a tight knot in my stomach as Franco's casket is lowered down next to his mother's. At least the gravesite reserved for him wasn't next to the father whose name he shouldn't have had, the father who wasn't his at all. It was next to his mother instead, whose mistake with his real father started all of this without her ever knowing the consequences it would have.

I can't help but glance across the cemetery towards the grave that I know is somewhere over there, where the Irish are buried. *Conor Macgregor.* The man whose last name Franco should have had.

Would things have been different? If his mother had come clean? She'd have been killed, probably, Franco given to some other family in a part of the country far from the offending Irish. It might have started a war, depending on how furious the cuckolded Bianchi husband was. But probably not. My father wouldn't have allowed that, I don't think. It would have been a humiliation, but one that was taken care of quietly.

Instead, it had been allowed to spin out of control. All because of one woman's lie.

It's hard for me to blame her as much as I might once have, though. I know what it's like now to lay next to a man that you not only don't love, but outright hate. I never met Franco's father, but I know it's possible that he was a cruel man too, that Franco's mother had been so desperate for affection, for love, for pleasure, that she'd made a mistake that could have cost her life. She'd been desperate enough to cover it up, too.

You can't change any of it. I watch as they lower the casket down, my hands clasped in front of me, and I remind myself of that over and over again. *It does no good to look back. Only forward.* I repeat it as I toss in the required handful of dirt, the white rose. I tell myself over and over again as I get back into the car to go home, a home that will shortly be full of people I'd rather not talk to, all expressing their sympathies for something that I'm grateful is over.

Just get through it. It's almost done. By tonight, I'll be free of it.

I've always been strong. My mother said I had a backbone of steel, but it's been sorely tested lately. Soon, very soon, I'll be able to let go.

What would my life look like, without the expectations of men?

I can't wait to find out.

* * *

The line of mourners wanting to speak with me and commiserate with me all over again is as endless as it was at the cathedral, but at some point between the *I'm so sorry's* and the offers of cookies and tuna casserole, I manage to corner Luca in the living room by the fireplace, a little ways away from the clustered groups of guests.

"How are you holding up, Caterina?" He looks at me with those intense green eyes of his, peering at me as if he can see the absolute truth of what I'm feeling. Maybe he can. Luca knows me well—better than Franco did, even. He was close to my father, after all. He helped arrange my betrothal. At one point, I'd wondered if I was going to marry *him*. I'd even asked my father about it, before I knew that he'd been promised to someone else, someone he'd never actually expected to ever marry.

Sofia, of course.

I'm glad that Luca isn't my husband. We wouldn't have been well-suited for one another, even less so than Franco and I were. But now he's in a different position altogether—one of power over me, as the don. And I'm more than a little afraid of what that might mean for me.

"As well as can be expected, I think," I say diplomatically, looking around the room. "I'm ready for some peace and quiet."

"Well, I'll get them out of your hair as soon as I can do so without creating a scandal," Luca says kindly. "My position does come with some perks, you know." He looks at me carefully. "I want to make sure that you're alright here alone, Caterina. That you—"

"I'll be fine," I say quickly. "I'm not fragile. I'm grieving, but I'll heal."

"No, you've never been fragile," he says, his voice thoughtful. "But you look as if there's something on your mind."

I pause, taking a breath. "We haven't spoken since—" I swallow hard, trying to think of the right way to say what needs to be said. "I want to apologize, Luca," I say formally, drawing my shoulders back as I look him squarely in the eye. "I had no knowledge of what my husband was doing, or what he had planned, but I was his wife nonetheless. I know that you might hold me somewhat responsible for all that happened. And I want you to know how very sorry I am for all of it, and that I wasn't able to stop it. That I was blind to my husband's betrayal of you."

Luca's eyes widen in shock, and he steps forward, gingerly putting his hands on my upper arms. I hate that I flinch at his touch—at any man's—but Sofia must have told him about the bruises, because his touch is exceedingly gentle. "Caterina," he says quietly, almost disapprovingly. "I don't blame you at all. How could you think that? Of course none of this was your fault. The fault was entirely Franco's and he's paid for it. You were his wife, but I had no reason to think that you were his confidant."

It's hard for me to entirely grasp the weight of what he's saying—I'm too overwhelmed by the events of the day still—but I feel relieved, nonetheless. I nod, blinking slowly as I grope for a nearby chair and sink into it, feeling as if I can breathe again. I hadn't realized just how worried I'd been until Luca said, aloud, that he didn't blame me in some way.

"But Caterina," he continues, his voice low and serious. It sounds far away, and I know that I've pushed past the point of what I can take for one day. I'm more tired than I've ever been, on the verge of passing out from emotion and sheer exhaustion, and I dimly see Sofia walking into the room, making her way quickly towards me.

"I do need something from you," Luca continues as Sofia walks to my side, gently helping me up. "For the good of the family, Caterina."

For the good of the family. How many times have I heard that over the course of my life? "Of course," I say numbly. "Whatever you need."

Purchase Captive Bride here.

ABOUT THE AUTHOR

Join the Facebook group for M. James' readers at
https://www.facebook.com/groups/531527334227005

ALSO BY M. JAMES

Vicious Promise

Broken Promise

Ruthless Promise

Captive Bride (coming soon)

Printed in Great Britain
by Amazon